The Eminently Forgettable
Life of Mrs Pankajam

Meera Rajagopalan is a writer based in Chennai. She 'sunlights' as a communications consultant for the development sector. Her fiction tends to veer around issues of identity and has appeared in several anthologies, including *Dissent: The Helter Skelter Anthology of New Writing Vol. 6* and *Have a Safe Journey*.

THE EMINENTLY FORGETTABLE LIFE OF Mrs PANKAJAM

Meera Rajagopalan

hachette
INDIA

First published in 2021 by Hachette India
(Registered name: Hachette Book Publishing India Pvt. Ltd)
An Hachette UK company
www.hachetteindia.com

SRD

ISBN 978-93-89253-89-4

Hachette Book Publishing India Pvt. Ltd
4th/5th Floors, Corporate Centre,
Plot No. 94, Sector 44, Gurugram 122003, India

Typeset in Bembo 11/17
by InoSoft Systems, Noida

Printed and bound in India by
Manipal Technologies Limited, Manipal

MIX
Paper from
responsible sources
FSC
www.fsc.org   FSC™ C043100

For Amma (Mine. Not the state's.)

Dear reader/voyeur,

Welcome to my diary.

First, to give credit where it is due, my counsellor put me up to the task of writing a diary. I quite enjoy the possibility of penning down my ideas and thoughts. No one listens to me anyway, while the paper looks like it won't object to my populating its pages with my thoughts.

My doctor keeps saying I need to talk about my feelings. Here goes, then. I've also been told I might be losing some memory, as if that is something I can prepare for.

In case this is found after I die, you might not want to waste your time reading it in its entirety before discarding it into the bin. I'm no Anne Frank.

I'm only a sixty-three-year-old lady from Chennai, aka Madras, writing about her uneventful life. I imagine it will mostly comprise the menu of the day and some family gossip. So if your taste buds don't tingle when you hear (read: read) *vathakuzhambu*,[1] you might as well burn this whole thing now.

---

1. Tangy, slightly sweet liquid; literally, sambar that is dried. Likely invented when a lady found out that the sambar had boiled a bit too much, and also that she had forgotten to boil the lentils. Perhaps she was chatting with a neighbour. Perhaps she was simply too tired.

Outside the ICU

Thursday, 3 April 2014

Srini had his second attack. It seems strange to start a diary like this, sort of *abasagunam*,[2] but I had to.

I heard Kamala tell Viswa, in whispers, that I made inappropriate jokes in the ambulance. What else was I to do? Srini was lying on the stretcher, and of course I didn't want to prolong the awkwardness and dampen everyone's spirits. It was a long ride, what with traffic and everything. Did they expect me to simply sniffle and/or cry and/or wail? The silence was too much, so I asked Kamala and her son a couple of riddles. Apparently, this is what considerate people receive as thanks – whispered gossip. For the record, they did not answer the riddles correctly.

The ICU is an entire storey to itself. The wait outside the ICU is a whole other story. It's like Russian roulette. You

2. Inauspicious. Mostly used for actions of girls and women: letting hair loose, combing hair after dark, sweeping the house after dark, and so on.

really have no idea what is happening within those chambers. Suddenly, one morning, when you walk in to relieve your daughter from her duties, you notice one family member is no longer present. Your daughter knows nothing about what's going on. You realize that they're either home, or Home. You're scared to ask anyone so you simply sit there, convincing yourself that they went back to their earthly home.

It's the same story every day, pretty much: we are all waiting outside for the doctor to enter the hallowed space of the ICU, and then for her to exit it. When she does, we ply her with questions that she hates to answer. This seems to be the attenders' schedule day after day. But during that wait, something else happens. Our relationships are peeled away, exposing us for who we are, and how. Here is where our relationships are weighed, and we are introduced to ourselves, in a manner of speaking. Don't they say that 'adversity does not build character; it reveals it' or something? How many times you check your phone, how you speak with your mother when your father is battling for his life, whether you stay overnight and sleep in that narrow chair (and do so timidly) – all these tell the stories of your life. You also make a quiet note of who called and who didn't, who came to the hospital and who didn't.

You check each other's wards' ailments and are suddenly aware of the organs that constitute us. You marvel, like a child, at how complex the human body is, and how your body, really, is not you but just a conglomerate of well-oiled systems whose presence, like good editing, you only notice when something goes bad.

I am mostly scared in places like this. New context and new places. It's like everything has changed or is constantly changing. See, a vacation is a change, but it's good: it has familiar people; a ~~death~~ patient at home is also bearable – same place, even if the context changes.

This hospital thing is terrifying. I'm clutching Srini's medical records so tight, my nails are tearing the folder. They have taken so many new tests, and I have also brought along his old test results. I constantly worry that I have left a crucial report back home – that one report that could mean the difference between life and...better life – as if these pieces of paper have left trails, like the breadcrumbs from a fairy tale, and even one lost breadcrumb could lead the doctors down the wrong path.

When we are allowed inside, the machines, the clean floors, the near-total sanitation is still bearable. What's unbearable is seeing the person you're there for – in a sense, they are not the same person outside the ICU. Like a coward, I hope that Srini is asleep so I can just take a peep and come back out.

I want his sarcastic comments, so that I can silence him. The silence without the attendant preamble is discomfiting. When I saw him lying there on the ICU bed yesterday, hooked up to all those tubes and machines, thinner than I had ever seen him, as if those tubes were actually slowly sucking life out of him, I desperately wished he wouldn't wake up right then and smile through his teeth, masking his pain. He has a talent for that. The beep-beeps I can yet handle, somewhat.

Thank God Viswa is here. She is my pillar of strength. She drove down as soon as she heard and has been here, doing everything. Pari called and asked if she should come but what would be the point? There wasn't enough work for two. I mean, for three. It has been Viswa all through – calling in favours, having friends contact doctors for second and third opinions, paying the money and holding me up. Sometimes, literally. She's been my Krishna. I sometimes hope she never leaves. But mostly, common sense returns and she irritates me.

This is Srini's second attack. Perhaps brought about by me.

You know how, when you resolve to do something, you are so diligent about it in the beginning? But in a few months (or days, in my case) things slip away, little at a time, almost imperceptibly, and you feel helpless about it? No matter how hard you try, like that frog in the well, you jump up only to slide back down? Imagine that over two years. That's what happened with Srini.

After the first attack, the menu at home would have put rabbits to shame. Slowly, festivals intruded and in the absence

4

of the children (Pari and Viswa, not the grandkids), it seemed like just one little diamond of Mysore pak would not make a difference, even if it were the best candidate for the title, 'The Widowmaker'. One more spoon of ghee would be okay. For what was the purpose of life if not to enjoy it in its entirety? What did we have to live for, we told ourselves, not failing to notice how the level of the philosophy we expounded was directly proportional to the number of dietary restrictions imposed. Slowly, coconut jostled its way into beetroot curry and fried *appalam*s muscled their way onto the plate.

It was just a regular early morning when it happened. I suppose I had just given Srini his coffee and he finished it, slurping his tongue as he usually did, indicating that he had finished and that I could take the tumbler–*davara* to the kitchen to rinse it. I was in the kitchen, cutting vegetables, when it happened. He called out for me, and clutched his heart.

In hindsight, Sorbitrate, his anti-cyanide, should have been in a locket on his neck. I once knew a man who actually kept it in a little watertight vial, suspended on his *poonal*. I laughed about it then, but now, it seems like genius. I got to his tablet bag, fished out the Sorbitrate and immediately placed it under his tongue. Then I breathed. I hoped it was just gas, like the last time we rushed to the hospital. I called an ambulance and it arrived not long after. By then, Srini had stopped clutching his heart and Kamala and her son had reached home and taken over some of the logistics. It was the first time I travelled in an ambulance; last time, I was parcelled off to Kamala's house ('Wait there, ma, till I call you,' Viswa had said). An ambulance ride is not like in the movies; in ours, there was a lot of talking about everything other than Srini, I now see, mostly by me.

Viswa, of course, immediately drove down from Bangalore. I felt relieved as soon as she entered the white corridors of the hospital, as if I had passed on the contentious box in a game of passing the parcel.

Sekar was already there (for his brother), but Viswa was the better choice to hold and take care of the parcel situation.

When the doctors suggested a bypass surgery, Viswa asked for a day to decide and sent the reports to all her doctor friends. She spent the entire night on the internet as I made Bournvita for her; it was like she was studying for her board exams all over again.

Palm Bella Vista, Chennai

Monday, 14 April 2014

Today is the Tamil New Year.

The girls called, as they have every single year they've been away. There's a list of days they call us on, a list that has remained constant for the past decade or so. The birthdays, anniversaries, New Year's, Gods' birthdays, I-Day, Deepavali, Pongal.

Ever notice how people wish you *Puthandu Vaazhthukkal* on 14 April and on 1 January, *Happy New Year*? As if the years lead parallel lives, like the audio tracks on those Magicbox DVDs I used to buy for Neel.

First up, at dawn, Pari called. The Angel.

Pari, Parineeta, whose dusky skin always was at dissonance with her name, causing eyebrows and inflections to rise. Even as a little girl her teachers would be puzzled, as if something did not quite add up and would ask her to repeat her parents' names, to confirm that a Pankajam and a Srinivasan actually came together to create a Parineeta. How do you explain with a straight face that your husband was so in love with the Bengali novel, that he decided on a name for your child while you were still floundering with the idea of being a parent?

Anyway, Pari called and wished us both Happy Tamil New Year, and we could even hear her drag her children to the phone. 'Come and talk to your paati and thatha and wish them. Right now!' we heard on speakerphone. 'We're just about to leave for a get-together, Amma,' she said, not explaining why the kids were awake, or where her husband, Siva, was. I can't recall when I spoke with him last. Months, perhaps.

The kids, lovely young free spirits, Neha, just two, and Neel, about eight, I think. I'd better be honest about my feelings: I cannot comprehend most of what Neel says on the phone, what with the thick American accent and the time difference. It's worse when he tries to talk like an Indian. Srini and I usually laugh nervously or repeat the last word as a question, if we don't understand what he says (which is almost always).

Sample this:

'Thatha, how's the weather there?'

We say, 'Weather there?'

'Paati, how are you?'

'You?'

8

When they visit India, at least we have visual cues. Never mind that Srini and I forever look like a pair of lemurs, gawking at his mouth. We could not, in good conscience, tell Pari that the phone was a terrible idea. We wished them both a happy new year.

Then came the call from Viswa, short for Viswapriya. She hated the full version of the name and insisted we not use it unless absolutely necessary. She was, in turns, Priya, Viswa, Vishy. She was supposed to have come home for New Year, but later said she had some work. I hope she has a boyfriend. Really. She is too picky for me to find a proper match for her.

She wants to move to Silicon Valley at some point, I think. It's about six hours from Silicone Valley, where all the Hollywood stars live! I read that in a book once. I thought it was funny. I've even written it down in my 'Lines for Thought' book. It's a collection of interesting lines and quotes from books.

Anyway, Silicon Valley is also where Pari lives. We've been there once, when Neel was born. There were nearly no foreigners in her area. I mean it's full of Indians and Chinese and Mexicans. Now, though, Pari and Siva have purchased a house in the outskirts. It must be with his money. I heard her say once that her teaching brought in next to nothing.

Srini showed me her house once on Google Maps. He clicked a button and the streets turned into housetops. We zoomed in as far as we could but could not see her or Siva. Then Srini told me the visuals were not live. 'She's not going to come out to the terrace and dry *vadam*s,' he said, and I wanted to wipe that smirk off his face. Sometimes he acts as if he is the professor from *My Fair Lady*. I mean, Kumbakonam is not London. And it's not so far from my Nandhimangalam. According to Google Maps, it's 62.3 kilometres.

Anyway, Viswa asked, as always, '*Enna samayal?*'[3] as if hearing the menu would somehow make her two-minute bachelor meals more palatable. A small detour (I can't seem to avoid them): Why does 'spinster' sound evil? Is it all the fairy tales? It sort of sounds like 'sinister' too, so I never use it. Maybe bachelorette? That sounds like kitchenette. Now I can't get the jingle out of my head – 'All is well and all is done with Nikitasha Kitchenette.' Does anyone remember that at all? Maybe I can ask Sekar.

Phone calls from the usual suspects must have followed – Sekar from across the city, my brother from Delhi. That is, not taking into account the numerous alerts from Srini's various WhatsApp groups.

As is custom, there was a movie on TV, apparently after 'only a few months in the theatres', as if that reflected positively on the said movie. Perhaps it does. The new always trumps the old, simply by virtue of being fraught with

3. What's cooking? (literally).

10

possibilities. That might be why other people like babies: the possible paths radiating from the baby are endless. But older people are set, like Mysore pak.

But I digress. I have no direction, so I digress from the narrative. I think that will suffice for the day.

Thursday, 24 April 2014

Voted. We were one of the first to go and vote – it was so easy. It's a secret ballot, so… Now the ballot boxes will be waiting for their delivery, pregnant with people's aspirations as they are. Come results day and we'll know if it's a boy or a girl! Or both!

Thursday, 1 May 2014

I don't know why we are not able to get Pari on the phone. I hope she and Siva and the kids are okay. The *sammandhis*[4] are not responding to our calls either. They haven't even

4.   Parents of the son- or daughter-in-law; a relationship based on well-masked mutual contempt for each other.

visited since Srini's attack. Sekar came home today, though, inquiring after his brother. He seems very frail, all of a sudden. Sekar, that is. Srini already is. I hope he is okay (Sekar). And also Srini, obviously.

Friday, 16 May 2014

I still haven't talked to Pari. I really do hope Siva's well. And she too. Absence may not make the heart grow fonder, but it sure makes it grow worried-er.

We have a new prime minister: Modi. And, of course, Amma is the chief minister. Amma and Modi.

Wednesday, 21 May 2014

I am having this form in front of me. I seem unable to complete this task. This form is for registration at Sri Sai Jathagalaya – a horoscope matching centre, for Viswa, and also for Prathik, Sekar's son.

So, this is what Viswa has asked me to look for in a boy:

• No more than two years' difference – older or younger.

- Equal or lesser educational qualification.
- Should not have been raised in Chennai. Should have lived outside Tamil Nadu for at least two years during his 'formative years' (whatever that means).
- Engineer okay, but not from all colleges (Encl: list of acceptable colleges).
- Should know how to cook. Should not expect her to know how to cook.
- Should be okay with prospective mother-in-law being interviewed (i.e. the boy's mother).
- List of hobbies cannot be 'watching movies, watching cricket'. If necessary, proof of said hobbies must be provided.

Prathik only wants 'a nice girl.'

Wednesday, 28 May 2014

Between Srini's check-ups and Viswa's horoscope/profile screening, I don't have enough time to even write this. And when I sit down to write, I feel I don't have anything to say. I feel like those kids, who, at every tourist spot, are so busy recording pictures, they forget to create memories. The picture, in effect, becomes the memory. This diary sort of feels like the camera that's recording useless pixels that trigger nothing. Something that says, like how some boys etch somewhere on a monument, 'Pankajam was here.'

For Viswa, it seems I am simply her secretary, passing on pre-screened profiles and photographs of boys who look as if they are about to be executed (they are, but they don't know it yet). I have to maintain another diary with details of all the boys and log their status. Srini has helpfully made me an Excel template and is encouraging me to use the computer for this. It's quite detailed. For example, options for 'Status' are: Profile, Photo, Horoscope, First meeting, Interview with in-laws, Interview with boy, etc.

We've had some good luck, though. Just yesterday we had quite a few phone calls for her, about her suitability as a woman who lights the lamp in the family. It was like asking the garden lizard about the fence, as a proverb goes. Or like asking the HR manager about a company. I dutifully extolled her virtues to the moon and back.

When I was to be married, all my father asked about Srini was whether he had a steady job (he did). That was it. Not even if he had a house, or what he planned to do with his life, nothing.

I can't imagine telling Viswa this. She would likely kill me. Matricide, it's called.

I finally asked Pari about Siva. She took a moment before she said she would ask him to call. I couldn't help but notice

14

the pause. I wonder why she couldn't just put him on the phone. He wouldn't avoid me, I know. We get along well. Like a house on fire, as they say. Maybe their house was on fire.

People think I don't notice things now that they feel my memory is peeling off, like the paint on this building. If anything, I think I notice better, because I have to. Like a half-blind person tends to peer longer at things. Also because I read books. I'm told it helps in staving off some of these geriatric mental problems.

Sunday, 1 June 2014

Things are getting back to normal, health-wise. Srini's leg pain is getting better, although his temper is not. Viswa has put me on some acupuncture treatment. Why me? I don't know. I think I'm the guinea pig. If I can handle it, they'll try it for the real patient: Srini.

I never knew needles could be so painless. So I lie down, and some twenty odd needles are poked into me as Srini looks on as if his dearest wish has come true. I lie, pin-laden (yes, Srini makes the joke), for about twenty minutes. Then the 'doctor' removes the pins and goes on his way. Sometimes, he leaves a couple of them in my body, and laughs when I mention it. How he can find it funny is beyond me! 'Doesn't matter, madam,' he says. 'It activates the nodes.' Maybe he means 'notes'. Anyway, I think I will stop this needles business soon. I don't think I need it. Nor do I think it's helping in any way. I don't even know what it is meant to improve.

Sunday, 8 June 2014

Srini's gone to the party they have organized here in the flats. They have one every year. It's usually at the clubhouse, but this year someone wanted a 'barbeque-style' party near the swimming pool. Like this is America or something. It's so hot.

He has already sent me many pictures from there. I don't like going down near the water. Not that I'm afraid or anything – I grew up next to a river, after all.

When I told my friends here, they thought I didn't know how to swim. Me, and not know swimming? I was nearly the champion swimmer in Nandhimangalam in my class, among the girls. If anything, it's the opposite: I feel a bit imbalanced physically, like something in the water will attract me, and that I'll go in. I am not joking. So I try and avoid large bodies of water. Or large bodies near water. I mean, I have to bathe and all that, of course.

Sunday, 15 June 2014

Viswa visits us every now and then, monthly visits, mostly to get her laundry done. And to refill on all the *podis*[5] I keep on the ready.

This time, she was happy (a rare occurrence): she was promoted and had to hire someone to work under her. I felt sad for the person at the other end of the line.

'Do you know the annual turnover of the company?'

'What do you think about paternity leave?'

'How long do you think reasonable work hours are?'

'Should spouses work in the same company?'

Questions like that.

When I heard the question that followed, I thought my daughter had lost her mind:

'Do you know how to bathe babies?'

Why was she asking about baby bathing? Maybe there was a point to it all. I remembered the time Viswa told us

5. Literally, powder. It has come to mean many things, including little, drugs, and some sort of black magic item. In this context, powder that can be mixed with rice to create palatable rice for the ultra-busy woman. Or the man who is forced to enter the kitchen.

about her job interview, where she was asked, apparently as an icebreaker, how the commute to the interview was. Not considering it part of the interview, she complained, as everyone is wont to, about traffic. She was rejected, just like that. It was, apparently, a test of her attitude: positive, sunny vs complaining, negative. More than 95 per cent of the country would fail this test, I think. Especially about traffic. And the government.

But bathing babies? What was she gauging? Adaptability to new technology? Working outside comfort zones? I looked on, and must have been staring at her, because she put the call on speakerphone.

The old lady who answered seemed just as taken aback: 'Yes, I do.'

Questions followed in quick succession. 'How religious are you?'

'Very.'

'Do you or your husband have any dietary restrictions?'

There was a short pause and a bulb went off in my head. This was her prospective mother-in-law!

Meanwhile, she was asking the lady, 'Who did you vote for?'

The lady at the other end of the line seemed to be teetering at the end of her tether. 'It's called a secret ballot for a reason,' she said tersely.

18

I waved my hands about, now desperate, trying to get her attention. She must stop this right now. What was she trying to understand? Secret-keeping abilities?

She looked at me, smiled, and simply handed me her list of questions. I wondered how I would fare if I were ever interviewed by Viswa.

While looking over the questions, all coded and bullet-pointed, I despaired. This prospective alliance seemed like a dead end. I dreaded another call from the mother of a boy telling me my daughter was too bold and aggressive and would never get married.

Right now, I mentally ticked off my answers:

What would you describe yourself as? Air or water? (Air)

What do you like? Test cricket, one-day or 20–20? (Test cricket, believe it or not. It keeps Srini occupied for days.)

Coffee or tea? (Coffee for me. 'Coffee or nothing,' the lady said. I liked this lady and did not wish my daughter on her.)

Kumudam or *Ananda Vikatan*? ('*Kalki*')

Serials or news? ('I don't watch much TV,' the lady said. She likely had a life.)

I wondered if the boy would get to ask me any questions. Srini naturally lapped it all up; his daughter was calling the shots! I refrained from taking him back decades, to what

I had asked him and his mother: Nothing. I hadn't even spoken to him until after we were married. And not much for years after either.

Sunday, 22 June 2014

We finally know what we suspected all along. At least what I suspected. Pari and Siva are having problems. Marital problems, as they say.

Viswa, on a trip to the US for work, told us this. Viswa didn't want to go to the US, actually, and offered to turn it down. But then, as I explained, Srini had just got new plumbing in his heart, and so the best time to go was now. That sounds so logical that it must be true.

I went to my neurologist this week and, apparently, I'm doing quite well. She said I might be experiencing some mood swings and ~~Sekar~~ Srini simply laughed at that. Imagine! Right in front of the good doctor. I didn't want to say anything and validate his point. So I kept quiet.

I'm reading again. Srini's doctors have asked him to keep away from aggravating things and I'm assuming I'm all of that one-item list. The best way to manage it is for me to curl up and read. The library here is abysmal, and I hope it improves as more people move in. When they do. If they do.

I remember the first book I read. Ammini and I sat by the riverbank. Ammini and I had always been best friends for as long as I can remember (which isn't saying much these days). She was short and stocky, the complete opposite of me, tall and thin as a reed. In complexion too: I was dark like the bark of the tamarind tree cut off to make space for the new school building, and she was fair like its inside. Her eyes were narrow little slits that seemingly pierced into your soul. In contrast, my eyes, I'd been told, were large, as if I were perpetually wonderstruck.

Ammini's mama had bought home an *Ambulimama* (we called it 'Amminimama') – it was so full of pictures and stories that we were amazed. Until then, we had never seen so many stories in one place, let alone an illustrated book. We had a small fight too. She wanted to read all the stories, and I wanted to wait and savour each one over time.

'We'll read one story a day,' I said, but she was adamant.

'Will anyone wait to enjoy stories?'

'But it will all be over.'

'Who knows what will happen tomorrow? I am going to read. You can go if you want to. I'll give you the book after I finish.'

I relented, of course, and we finished the book in one stretch. *Ambulimama* had everything: kings, queens, faraway lands, magic and a generous dose of stories from China and Turkey and suchlike – places we couldn't even point out on a map. Parched, we devoured it all in one gulp. And as I'd predicted, afterwards we didn't have any more. So we re-read the book several times, waiting for Ammini's mama to visit again, but strangely that never happened until, well, ever. Alas, the horizons of Nandhimangalam were not vast enough to accommodate reading for pleasure. Nor were my mother's. Not that it mattered much then.

I only hope that wherever she is now, Ammini is reading to her heart's content.

Sunday, 29 June 2014

I've been good, and have written every week, I see. I'm proud of myself.

I forgot to write about the most important thing that we have been talking about: Pari and Siva are not together. Somehow, it seems sort of natural. Like Rajini movies, which are exciting, but overall you know the road it's going to take and the destination. I don't know when I started thinking that about Siva and Pari. Or maybe it was always just there, just below the surface, like long-held prejudice.

Viswa called last week. She told me to put her on speakerphone.

'Amma, Appa, something important.'

We waited eagerly, our lives tethered to our daughters' through these invisible waves.

There was a pause. Too much of a pause. Perhaps it was Viswa's time to take centre stage and she wanted to extend it, like when they literally had to drag Ammini off stage even after she, as Tiruppur Kumaran, was dead, clutching the Indian flag on her chest.

'*Avan inga illa, ma.*' She used the colloquial form to address him. As if he were a retired official who had lost access to the honorific bungalow. As it turned out, it was exactly that.

'Huh?'

'It is as if Siva was never here. I was even a bit scared, Pa. Photos, clothes, everything's gone.'

Why was she addressing him? *I* had picked up the call.

'What is she saying?' I asked.

'They have separated. The kids are with him over the weekend and with her during the week.'

'Separated means?'

'Maa. Pch.'

'So they can reconcile? Why hasn't she told me?'

'Pa, must be because of your attack. Anyway, she says she doesn't want to talk about it.'

'Even to you?'

'Of course to me too, Pa. If she didn't talk to you, how will she talk to me?'

'That's also correct.'

23

Yes, it was so natural, her order of preference.

This is a new phrase – not wanting to talk about something painful. Of course one doesn't. It's like me saying, I don't want to get this baby out; it's too painful! Even if it's a thirty-hour delivery, it has to be done. Even if Srini jokes that I was like the Boat Mail making an overnight delivery, and Sekar laughs that irritating laugh that makes my hair stand on end, it's not like I had a choice.

'So what are they going to do?'

I could feel her shrug. 'God knows. She seems quite okay, really. So maybe it was a good thing.'

'Wonder what the fellow did. You think it was an affair? How could he?'

I nearly chortled. Srini, always protective of his little girl. Truth be told, Pari never needed much mollycoddling. She was the older sibling and if anything, she was protective of all of us, even her father. When she got married, all our relatives were worried that she would display too much of her independence. Her best friend and cousin, Preethi, apparently told her just before her wedding to Siva, 'Show some vulnerability, so that Siva can feel like he is taking care of you.' We had laughed about it then. Now I was thankful for Pari's steadfastness and independence. But surely, we couldn't just shift the blame onto the poor boy.

'Come on,' I had to interject. 'You know nothing about the situation. Maybe it was she who had an affair?'

I could feel the air sucked out from around me. Really, though, if you saw the two of them together, impartially, like I did, that's exactly what you would think. I wasn't exactly sure why Viswa seemed shocked at this possibility. It wasn't as if she was biased towards her sister. Why, when they were kids, she would make up such wild stories about her sister that Srini would simply ignore them.

She could say, 'Appa, Pari killed a boy in class,' and Srini would say, 'I'm sure he took her pencil.'

Viswa, having passed on the information, must have felt like a telephone wire.

'Okay, I have to go,' she rushed.

'Are you okay, ma?'

'Yes, Pa. Thanks for asking.'

'Take care. Eat well.'

Srini looked at me. If only he gave me an opening to actually talk. Before I could say anything, Viswa said, 'Bye, Pa. Bye, Ma,' and hung up.

Srini was quiet for a long time and I was worried. I shook his shoulder and he seemed to come out of whatever trance he was in.

'She'll be okay, right?' I asked him – one of those questions with only one correct answer.

He did not answer immediately. I don't recall ever seeing him so shaken up. Almost. I look back at the two of them, Srini and Pari, and all I remember is them as a team, nearly inseparable. The two of them, always conspiring, forever talking in secret code, a little something that held them together, like twins in a single placenta. As long as I was providing the nourishment via snacks.

One evening, Pari must have been thirteen, maybe, when the two of them were sitting on the steps leading up to our one-bed portion. In their hands was a piece of a stem of the hibiscus plant. Pari was taking the flower apart and showing Srini the different parts of the plant. He listened carefully and then seemed to ask her a question. She seemed to answer emphatically. All his attention was on her. I know that look – I've never been at the receiving end of it. The entire time their hands held the stem. At that exact moment, Viswa came home from playing and tried to bulldoze her way between them, even tickling Pari, but they would not budge. Instead, Pari leaned to her right so Viswa could climb up the stairs. There was a flash of anger on Viswa's face that seemed to be directed, of all people, at me. Pari had not broken her conversation with her father for even a beat, and they continued.

All those years ago, when Pari brought Siva home, he had not batted an eyelid. He had only asked her, 'Are you sure?'

In her characteristic style Pari admonished her father. 'Appa, of course. Do you think I'd bring him home if I were not?'

'Okay,' Srini had said, as Pari sought to assuage his feelings.

'I know I'm a bit unconventional, but Siva knows me and likes me for who I am, Appa. All those guys you parade in front of me have no idea about me. Siva knows me and we are friends first. That's important, no?'

Now, that son-in-law was out of our lives. After fifteen years of living on the periphery of our lives, he was out of our orbit. When Srini spoke, finally, I heaved a sigh of relief. 'Finally, she got rid of that good-for-nothing fellow,' he said. 'She is worth so much more.'

I remained silent.

'I hope she finds someone worthy of her,' he continued.

For him, I wondered if anyone would ever be.

Sunday, 6 July 2014

Viswa calls every day on Skype. We kind of like it, but still, every day? My days are pretty routine — any deviation is rare and infinitesimally important. She doesn't even call at the same time every day, so her call is sometimes the only occurrence that doesn't follow a schedule.

When she called today, I was in Kamala's house getting ready for our class. It's not like a proper class. Her grandchildren were around and Kamala heaved herself up to go give them their mid-morning snack. 'What is this eating six times, like a pregnant woman? Just feed the kids twice,' I said. 'All this mid-morning, mid-afternoon, midnight snacks are making them fat.'

I saw she had brought some Lay's chips, but I kept my own counsel.

Just as she started talking about what her daughter-in-law did last night, the bell rang and Kavitha walked in saying, 'You won't believe what happened!' Kavitha always has great trailers, but the movies rarely match up.

That was when Viswa chose to call. 'Viswa Daughter calling' Skype says, her deer-in-the-headlights photo pulsing within the circle. (Srini has saved her as Viswa Daughter on my phone and as Viswapriya on his. And Pari, of course, on his phone is P. As if she's MS. Or MGR.)

I swipe red and instantly feel guilty also. Will Viswa know I rejected her call?

I know Srini taught me how to silence it, but I just can't seem to remember how.

Somehow, new information does not seem to stay in my head for too long. I think that's what my condition is. 'That's because my brain is so full,' I told Srini the other day.

'Yeah, full of yourself,' he retorted. It was clever, and I noted it down. It might be good to use somewhere.

There was no time to dwell on these things because we had new stories to catch up on. I haven't yet told them about Pari. I have more questions than answers.

We finally got down to chanting the *Laliltha Sahasranamam*. That's what we do. In fact, our WhatsApp group name is Bella Bhakti Group, even if the slokas sometimes feel like a footnote. We also do slokas. Like the Tata Steel ad.

Friday, 15 August 2014

I feel the need to record important days, for some reason. I think I've taken a long break from writing in this. I got up early to watch the prime minister's speech. It felt good to watch someone talk about things that mattered. But soon, it got repetitive. He spoke about open defecation, and I cringed. While I knew my friends would pooh-pooh it and cluck their tongues at the poor women who had to undergo this ignominy, I knew I wouldn't be able to bring myself to declare my antecedents: in Nandhimangalam, that's what we did. The first time I used a proper toilet was at a function in Trichy. That too was not a toilet as you would imagine: it was just a hole-in-the-floor where the offending substances collected at the bottom. I wondered how they cleaned it but was also afraid to ask. Flies buzzed around and you couldn't sit on the two raised pieces of stone for a long time, reading a magazine like we do today in our gleaming white Western toilet. So, yes, I knew how it was, and knew it would be great if women had toilets in their homes. It would have been great if someone had thought of it thirty years ago, but well, what can you say?

In other news, no clarity is emerging on the Pari situation, although we've been thinking about it a lot. She hasn't yet told us anything about why she and Siva are no longer together. Can she not understand that we need to know? We went on Facebook to search for clues. We've become seasoned detectives, what with unlimited internet and time on our hands. But disappointingly, Pari's Facebook page held no answers. She wasn't on it much and had only recently uploaded some pictures from her childhood. There were some Deepavali party pictures from last year too, where she looks pretty in a purple ghaghra. She looks like a replica of Srini, if I could imagine him in a dress called a ghaghra! In one of the pictures she has her arm around her friend's shoulders and looks straight ahead at the camera. I thought I spotted Siva in the background, but I couldn't be sure. She looked happy enough and we took it, literally, at face value.

Finally, Viswa is back in India and all we wanted to know was about Pari. Srini and I were impatient. What had happened? Was the marriage salvageable? Or should we just flick it all away and start afresh? Was it another girl that Siva had? Or another man? Or had she killed him off and buried him in the basement, like *Nooravadhu Naal*? What was it?

Viswa laughed. 'Let me be for a bit. This is too much!' she said and retreated to the kitchen, milking her two minutes of fame.

'Viswapriya,' Srini's voice boomed. 'You will come here and talk to us. Right now!'

Even I was taken aback by that tone. I had never heard him so angry before.

Viswa, though, seemed unperturbed. She ran her hands through her gorgeously wavy hair, trying to bring a semblance of order to it. She picked an apple from the fridge and sauntered back into the hall to sit opposite her father.

Srini's face darkened further, if that were even possible.

Viswa bit into the apple. The crunch echoed in the hall. 'Appa,' she began, 'it's nothing big. You please don't get tension.'

'If anyone tells me one more time not to get stressed, I will simply blow up,' he said calmly.

'Wait, wait,' I said, and had to physically intervene, my back towards Srini.

'Come on, Viswa, you know how things are. We are also stressed out,' I said. 'It's not as if you are protecting either of us, or your sister. Appa's heart is not the issue here, Pari's life is.' I keep supplying them the logic about the new arteries, about it being new plumbing and therefore clear, but no one is buying it. I must get this theory vetted by Dr Aadhavan when we go in next. See, everyone wants a doctor's stamp on opinions.

I sat down. Viswa slowly told us what she had gleaned from her two visits to her sister's house. It's still not clear, she said, as to what has happened between them. Pari seemed happy enough, going out for dinner and drinks with her friends, at least when Viswa was around. The children spend most weekends with their father and are adjusting to the new situation better than she thought they would. Pari did not talk much about it, but the children did, she said. They had told Viswa about their dad being away for a long time.

'How is she?' I asked, and Viswa shrugged.

'What does that mean?' I demanded.

'She's...as usual. You know she's strong. I was the one who was feeling sad. She seemed absolutely fine. Happier, in fact.'

That seemed to satisfy Srini. 'Maybe she just needs some time. We'll give it to her. If anything, I know my daughter can face any challenge.' My daughter. As if he had reproduced by simply pinching off a part of himself, like an amoeba. Where was the 'we'? But I let it pass, keeping the larger picture in mind.

That night, as I lay in bed, Srini asked me: 'She will be okay, right? What do you think happened?'

I was almost sure she'd kicked Siva out because she didn't have the patience for him, or he for her. Or she might have fallen in love again. I didn't think that last statement would sit well with Srini, pristine as his daughter's image was supposed to be. She was, after all, the angel. It is, by the way, so difficult to get an angel's costume for fancy dress. Invariably it has some stain or other. Srini would tell a sulking Pari that the moon too had its stains. Then she would relent.

'I don't know what happened, Srini. But I know that if anyone can stay above water, it's her.'

He sighed with relief and turned, as he always did, the other way. In five minutes, he was snoring.

I tried to remember my daughter as I saw her last and found the visual memory slipping. I could not remember clearly how my own daughter looked. This was very frustrating. I opened up pictures on the computer and stared at them for a long time, as if I could remember if only the image was impressed in my brain a bit longer. Then I closed my eyes and tried again. It worked for a bit.

Srini believed with all his heart that Siva was the 'culprit'. I worried that I didn't. Surely Pari didn't say why she separated because *she* was the one to ask for it? If Siva had done something, she would have told us. She was walking on eggshells around Srini. Perhaps she would respond better to me, precisely because I sought information, not emotion?

I sense that something is wrong with the whole situation. None of our explanations sit right, there's something awkward like an almost-right jigsaw piece. We have to keep looking. It's like watching shadows from behind a translucent *veshti*, and wishing it would simply be removed.

Monday, 1 September 2014

I'm sitting on a plane as I write this. Srini keeps trying to peep but I won't let him. Amazing wonders; the seat next to me is empty! Perks of travelling to the US during the off season. The old birds are usually migrating in the opposite direction.

It just happened, this trip. When you're older, you just want to relax, not worry about your kids. They're not even kids any more. You want to hold your grandchildren in your arms, play with them and pass them back to your children when they do their business. You don't want to be doing much, aside from giving your opinion. The most you want to do is advise and act hurt when your advice is ignored.

I wish my kids would understand that. Tell us your worries; we are not made of glass. Don't make us do things; we are not made of steel.

I guess I need to rewind a bit. The Pari situation is still unresolved, in the sense that we don't know much. She has forbidden us from speaking with Siva's parents, and we follow. I emailed her, asking her if she would like to tell me what happened, and all I got was a cryptic, 'All in good time.' She had added a CC to Srini, who stared me up and down the next morning. I ignored him completely.

Just last week, Srini suddenly asked, 'Why don't we go meet Pari?'

We have a standing invitation from her, to visit the US whenever we want. More importantly, we have one of those ten-year visas that mean we don't have to stand in line and stress about it a lot.

So, just like that, we are bound for America. On a stuffy plane to London and thence to San Jose. Who says 'thence' any more?

I have so much time on the plane and the movies don't interest me. Surely this is a scientific statement: because movies are all over the place, and on demand, but they are not as good as they were earlier.

Clicking the download button can never match up to entering the dark *kottagai*, sitting on the sand spread out especially for *tharai* tickets, and whispering loudly, excitement fuelled by the posters brought around on bullock carts to the entire village, can it? It was ages earlier that Ammini and I watched that great movie forever etched into the Tamil mind:

Veerapandiya Kattabomman. What acting! Ammini and I held each other and cried when the movie ended, even as her brother, Mani, who was our chaperone, made fun of us.

'You are crying about a hundred years too late,' he said, and we shot daggers at him.

We sobbed all the way back home, our tears tying us stronger together. Never have I felt so moved since. A movie is not just what's on the surface or the screen, it's the experience. Like family.

The United States of America

Thursday, 4 September 2014

We've landed and we've mostly just been asleep. I dream of India and when I wake up, I'm all confused. I don't know where I am. I expect Aavin milk in the fridge and curd set in a stainless-steel vessel. Not several-days-old milk in a can and curd out of a plastic tub. In one corner of her *medai*[6] lies the coffee maker. The one that gurgles and spews out steam and coffee. I'd packed a coffee filter in my hand luggage, just in case. And of course, it's case.

After the Bella apartment and the flight, Pari's house is how schoolkids feel when they have a games period. I find myself taking deeper breaths here. It's as if everything has ballooned, like idli *maavu*, and instantly become lighter. I feel younger, faster, and maybe, just maybe, I'll have better memory. It is all in the mind, they say!

6. Literally, stage. Also, specifically the kitchen counter, for where else can women perform best?

We haven't yet spoken with Pari, and she told us right off the bat that once we're settled in, we'd talk. She said a friend is coming home for dinner tomorrow. It must be her new boyfriend. White, maybe? She wouldn't want to go back to another Indian man, I think. Makes sense to go full opposite. Although, black would be opposite too. Brown is the centre of the colour scale. I wonder how Siva is doing. We must call him.

Neha and Neel are going to Siva's house after school tomorrow. They'd made us 'Welcome' cards, which was very sweet. They had grown, I said, although I had no memory of their height from two years ago. They seemed okay, and were laughing, and we didn't ask them about Siva. I was glad that their parents' break-up had not affected them as much as I had feared.

Thought, actually, not feared. Somehow they were so removed by distance, time and daily routine that I had not allowed myself to worry about them. Honestly, I think the reason is that I don't know them. I know Siva's parents better than I know these two. What makes them happy? Sad? Angry? Who do they like? How are they when they fight? Does Neel give in, mostly, or does Neha? Does Neel share what happens in school? In the playground, is Neha the one who cuts the line to the slide, or is she the one who gets cut? I had no answers to any of these. The weekly calls where they repeated answers to questions like trained parrots hadn't offered any insights. I suppose that's what distance does to you. You don't follow a person through their evolution — so you're expecting a Neanderthal, but looking at a Homo sapiens.

Friday, 5 September 2014

The Sword of Damocles has fallen. We had a nice dinner, where it was all explained. I should have known the topic would be broached the minute Pari suggested she would make a nice dinner. She never cooks if she can help it.

The kids were packed off to their father's. A father whose very existence we found Pari had erased. The kids were giggling as they left.

So, when the bell rang, close to 7 p.m., I was all dressed up in my Kanchivaram sari, the deep blue one with the maroon border, waiting to greet who I hoped would be a tall and handsome American man. When I opened the door, though, there was no man, tall or short, staring down at me and breaking into a huge smile. There was a woman instead, heavy set, puffing and panting as if she had run the marathon. And Indian-looking. She could have passed for one of those South American types, but something told me she was Indian. Perhaps it was her kurti with mango designs, paired with blue jeans. It looked familiar, the kurti.

'Hello, Aunty,' the woman said, and I nearly blocked the entrance. What was this woman doing? I prayed Pari would not let her stay for dinner. Whatever she wanted, she better get it and leave quickly. Was it salt? Sugar? Maida? Middle-class worries, I later realized.

'Pari,' I called out urgently.

My daughter came to the door and smiled at the newcomer. There was a pause and then they exchanged a look, a look that made me feel like I was interrupting something. I immediately moved away, retracing my steps to the living room sofa.

There was something there, I knew, and glanced over at Srini. His finger, for once, was not on the phone screen. As I followed his gaze, it led me to a moment frozen in time. Pari and the woman were kissing, just a gentle peck, but it was enough. It was the key to the seemingly random cryptogram. The random events and thoughts and feelings in Pari's life now clicked neatly into place, like a well-written Agatha Christie mystery.

Funnily, I remember everything about that moment – it's like a photograph I can return to.

I remember twisting the ring around my finger, that I'd placed one leg above the other, that I was facing the door, with Pari's back to me, and that Srini was in the single-seater sofa opposite me. I remember the prick of the blue-and-red gold covering set from Narayana Pearls on my neck, reminding me of my odd obsession with the weddings of my two daughters and attendant expenses. I remember being reminded, in passing, of how Srini's aunt had forbidden more kids, as if it were a collective decision of random family members, saying, 'You're already at minus two. What if you don't get a plus this time around too? Minus three, with one income, you'll go bankrupt.'

I remember my gaze sweeping across the room, pausing at the framed painting of a lovely young woman holding a lamp, to the right of the door, while watching over Pari and the girl. I remember thinking, incoherently, that it seemed as if the light on their faces came from the lamp. I remember the chill of the early winter air making its presence known on my face.

But most of all, I can remember the smile on Pari's face.

Monday, 8 September 2014

Today is Monday. The first weekday after it all went down. Somehow, I feel at peace.

Everything circles around Friday, the dinner.

I can't understand it, but it doesn't bother me much. I can't really explain it, but it's as if everything is in its state of rest. The way that seems natural. Sometimes, I see *mamis* here in America wearing jeans and shirts. I know that's not them, and they know it's not them either. It was as if Pari had taken off her jeans and shirt and finally draped herself in a sari.

What I wonder about most is how she fell in love and got married to Siva in the first place. I also wonder how he is doing. The dinner was a sombre affair with Pari introducing us to Radha as her friend. Radha seemed to be, by turns, embarrassed and amused.

Srini, of course, had been quiet the entire evening, and I had been trying to completely ignore the white elephant (or is it pink?) in the room. Pink would make more sense, I suppose. You would have to be mad not to notice it.

Pari slowly began a conversation amid the quiet clatter of cutlery. 'Appa, Amma, there's obviously something very important I need to tell you guys.'

Srini snorted.

Pari shot him a look, a mixture of pity and sadness that I don't wish on anyone.

'I've been preparing to say this for a long time, and I will say it.'

Radha, who was sitting next to her, held her hand and squeezed it, and Pari, incredibly, simmered down, as if Radha's hand were a wet cloth thrown on a hot cooker.

'Appa, Amma, this is who I am. A lesbian.'

Srini looked away, as if it were an airborne infection. Such a village reaction he has sometimes.

She continued, 'First, this does not change anything. I am still your daughter. This does not mean that I have suddenly become a boy.'

Srini did not look at her. His mouth was contorted, and his gaze was still fixed at an indeterminate spot on the floor. The soup Pari had made was really very good, I must say. She has learned quite a lot of cooking, it seems.

'It's not new, either. You know we've been around forever. Appa, you were the one who told me about this – that there are many such stories in our Puranas. And it continues. In fact, remember, Amma, you told me about your cousin sister who would hide and stare at you girls when you were bathing in the river?'

I did. It was another Radha, actually. Radhalakshmi. My *mama*'s daughter, six years older than me. She was married off, and her husband had a 'keep' and we all wished the worst on that fellow. Eventually, Radha committed suicide.

I shuddered.

'Amma, somehow, I always felt you knew. Even when I brought Siva home.'

43

I was startled. I knew? No, madam, I did not, I wanted to say, as Srini turned to me.

'Yes, Amma. Remember, you asked me thrice, "Are you sure?" when I introduced you to Siva? Surely you knew there was something off about it all.'

I do remember that day, but I had never in a million years thought my daughter was a lesbian. Through the short haircuts, through her sort of disinterest about men until Siva came along, through her years in the hostel when I discovered letters to a 'Shailu darling' in her room, I had never considered it. I suspect she hadn't either.

'Sexless' was the default for girls until they were married, after which they were to consummate like crazy; there was no need for anyone to assume otherwise.

If she thinks I had some sixth (or seventh) mother's sense that everyone talks about, I wasn't going to out myself. Srini, of course, was shaking his head.

'What did I do? What did I do?' he kept repeating slowly.

Pari looked at her father, her hero, his eyes lowered in shame.

'It wasn't you, Pa,' she said softly. 'This has nothing to do with you.'

Srini remained silent.

'I'm serious, Pa,' she said, walking to where her father was seated, his eyes not leaving the floor, like a shy bride. She knelt by him.

Calmly, she took his hands in hers. 'Appa, listen. It doesn't really change anything. Please don't worry. I am still your Pari, the one who can make you laugh and cry in a single breath.'

That again. I had heard that so many times when she was growing up. I'd challenge her to do that, but this hardly seemed the time.

'Who are you? My daughter? Or son? What are you? And what about this...this person here? What is she? He? Who is the man here? You? Her? Him? What is all this? No one in our family does this. My mistake, sending you so far from home with that Siva. Look what he has done to you.'

I'll say this again: poor Siva. Really. Imagine sharing more than your life; sharing an interest in women. I remember Viswa telling me about this show she watched on TV with exactly the same premise. I can't remember it now, though it was a simple word.

I wondered what Viswa was doing now, and hoped she was regular. Hetero. Straight. Whatever's the right term. Or at least that she has it figured out.

On Sunday, I felt a need to speak with Siva, to reach out to the poor man whose world must have been shattered one night like this. Or perhaps over several nights, tossing around in their marital bed, unsure, devoid of pleasure. I must say, these things come suddenly. These flashes of poetry.

I fret about why I'm not more upset or bothered about the whole thing. It seems like I'm worried about everything other than Pari. That's got to be good, right?

Or do I just not care? Am I extremely open-minded? Am I evolved? I have no idea. Perhaps it is because I read a lot. In books there are characters of all hues, especially grey. Nothing's ever black or white, so you read, understand, accept. When you live with them in your head, you sort of go through the entire gamut of emotions on their behalf. Is that it?

At least one thing I'm not worried about are my grandchildren. They came back home after school on Monday, and it was obvious they already knew. It didn't seem like a big deal to anyone.

I felt adventurous and sent the news to my Bella Bhakti Group. Dead silence.

Tuesday, 9 September 2014

The house is eerily quiet, the air beyond-due-date pregnant with words that can't yet be delivered. The kids are up and about, their new schools, friends and everything else taking up space, pushing the unspoken even further down.

Srini and I have not yet really broached the topic with Pari since. We are middle class. We don't talk about emotions and all that, not unless it is absolutely necessary.

Even that night, after Radha left, Pari asked her father, 'Well?'

'Well, what?'

'Well, Appa, is it a big shock? Are you okay?'

'Okay? Okay? How can I be okay?'

She then turned to me as if she were a waiter taking our orders at a nice restaurant: 'You, Amma?'

I shrugged. 'Okay.'

We called Viswa and I told her what had happened. She shrieked and was a little too shocked, truth be told. I think she registered a near 8.0 on the Richter scale. She would make a good replacement for Jyothika in movies. Srini was taken in by her performance, I think, and he was somehow satisfied that he had company.

That was it. We went on like it was business as usual. Personal as usual. Whatever.

It was exactly how we dealt with Ammini, when she left. She was there one day and gone the next. I was struck by how easily mentions of her had been replaced everywhere: in school, at dinner and in our lives in general. Now it seemed Radha had been added, in much the same way.

Monday, 15 September 2014

It seems that the house has started to breathe, has been returned to its rhythm. Pari left us alone on Saturday night, all decked up. We didn't ask; she didn't tell. When she left, I asked Srini (again) what he thought of all of this. He had been awfully quiet since that night.

As usual, he snorted and went back to his phone. As usual, I wanted to thwack him on the head with it.

So, of course, I WhatsApp-called Sekar, the next best thing to do.

I don't recall much of the conversation, but it went something like this:

'Sekar. *Oru* news.'

'*Enna, manni?* Good news?'

'I have no idea.'

'What do you mean?'

'I don't know how to say this. I will just tell you. Siva and Pari are divorced.'

'Oh no. He was a good guy, no?'

'Yes, yes, he still is.'

'Then?'

'It's something else.'

'What?'

'She has found someone else.'

'Ah, not his brother...'

I added, too quickly, 'A girl. She's seeing a girl.'

'Seeing means?'

'*Adhaan*. Girlfriend.'

I did not hear anything from him for a long time. I thought we were disconnected. Turns out that he was processing the information.

'Sekar?'

A few sharp breaths later, he responded. 'Yes, I'm here. How are you all doing?'

'It's not a funeral, Sekar. It took some getting used to, but we are fine.'

'How is *anna*?'

He is just fine, thank you, I wanted to scream. 'Anyway, how are you doing?'

There was another pause. It seemed the phone was handed over. To Renuka, his wife. I could imagine her, pleats perfectly in place, gingerly taking the phone from Sekar. Renuka was Pankajam[-1]. It was as if, after me, he had decided he wanted the exact opposite for himself, and had gone and brought Renuka into the family. Years later, Renuka and I were still formal with each other. I've never even thought of calling her Renu.

'He is not doing well, *manni*.'

49

'What?'

'Yes, they have taken his tumour for biopsy again. One test came back positive.'

'Biopsy-na? Positive-na?' I must have been shouting.

'Cancer,' she sobbed into the phone.

I could not think for a minute. I handed over the phone to Srini. Then I ran into the kitchen, leaned on the island, as they call it, and sobbed.

Tuesday, 7 October 2014

I seem to have missed several weeks of writing. I don't remember what we ate yesterday. My head doesn't feel right. But I remember that we spoke to Siva. He has invited us to dinner some time. I would really like that. Maybe I initiated it... actually I am sure I did because Srini was very worried about meeting him.

Tuesday, 14 October 2014

Renuka called. Sekar is being taken in for chemotherapy. They said they detected it early; that's got to mean it can be cured, right? Stomach, she said. Google tells me the recovery rate is not so great. That's only statistics. He could be one of those who beats the statistics. He would be. He has to be.

He's like the hum of the refrigerator in my life's kitchen.

The first time I saw him, I did not know who he was – he looks nothing like Srini, plus no one really introduces women to anyone, at least in India. He had not come to the girl-seeing, and I had not gone to my engagement. I first saw him at the *nalangu*, after the wedding. Usually around four o'clock, after the wedding lunch and after everyone has had some rest (except the girl's parents, who are spinning around like tops forever), everyone gathers around for some traditional games that the couple plays: wresting a coconut from the other's grasp, finding a ring in a pot of milk, smashing *appalam*s over each other's heads, etc. Both sides cheer for their candidate, and it's meant to be practice for the give-and-take that marriage will inevitably entail.

It's also a space for old folk to tease the young couple and crack flat, double-meaning jokes. As I sat there, waiting for the older ladies to set everything up, I looked around – my cousins sat near me, ready to egg me on to win. In front of me was a man I barely knew. I was already nervous about the night. Next to him were two other men, looking directly at me.

51

When the games began, I realized that Srini did not try very hard. It seemed as if he would not mind me winning every game (and there were a lot of them). The man next to him, though, would not let him.

'*Ennanna*, you are letting her win everything?' Sekar asked him. 'Is this the future?' he mocked. When Srini continued, Sekar did the unthinkable: before anyone could realize it, he grabbed the coconut himself.

'Now try,' he challenged, and I, only schooled to obey a male voice, tried to.

There was a collective hush that seemed to persist for a long time. I took the opportunity, when he looked around, seemingly clueless, and wrested the coconut away from him in a split second. 'My' side roared in solidarity.

My cousin whispered in my ear that the impertinent young man was my brother-in-law. 'Ask your mother-in-law if they are looking for girls for him,' she giggled into my ear.

I barely heard her. So this was the brother-in-law I would be living with.

After I was brought to what would eventually become my home, I got to know its people better. It was nearly a week before all the auxiliaries left and the 'normal household' remained: me, Srini, Sekar and my mother-in-law.

As I tried to fit in, I was reminded of how, years earlier, my brother had brought home a puppy against everyone's wishes. The puppy had sniffed around everywhere and tried to figure out the pecking order. I kept returning to that time as I looked around for vague clues on how I should act. Some things immediately caught my eyes: the pile of magazines strewn around. The towel carelessly thrown on the clothesline. A dinner plate left on the dining table. All of this was Sekar's doing. Srini was a study in contrast: immaculately dressed, clean shaven, clothes neatly folded in the cupboard. It should have been a relief that he did not depend on me for his everyday needs – but somehow, it was irritating.

It was as if our bedroom was the refuge and a storm raged outside; yet, I wanted to be with the storm. Not to be outdone, I pored over the magazines too, strewing them around even more. All the time I bombarded Sekar with questions: his favourite series, characters and novelists. We discussed these at length, much to my mother-in-law's irritation. I remember how we argued, fought over and discussed serialized novels: Jayakanthan's words were shredded apart as if they'd been eaten by a bulldog. We would fight for the week's *Ananda Vikatan* and *Kalki*, to discuss the stories in them, week after week. How Sekar had thundered when I said that Jayakanthan's novels, especially the then-all-the-rage *Sila Nerangalil Sila Manithargal*, were worth nothing but shock value!

'You take that right back!' he had said, as I stood resolutely by my opinion.

'I will not eat food in this house until we settle this!' he said and left that day.

In the mean time, I took out all my bound novels, and annotated the text as if it were an assignment. I painstakingly copied passages to make my point.

I still remember one of them. 'Ganga is nothing but a cut-out. For if Jayakanthan really wanted to free her, he would have paired her with someone, even someone who knew about her past. In keeping her tied to Prabhu, he is not talking of any liberation.' Or words to that effect.

When Srini came home and made the mistake of asking us what had happened, we both snapped at the same time, 'Be quiet!'

Srini, in all his goodness, thought two copies of the magazine would help. He didn't know what hit him when we pounced on him instead.

Even today, my mind can conjure up an image of Sekar leaning on the sturdy writing desk in his study room, and me, speaking aloud from the kitchen, so that the whole house reverberated with the echoes of my opinions.

'What devil has possessed this girl!' my mother-in-law would say, and Sekar would act as my microphone.

'Why? Even reading is wrong?'

'*Ennavo po*. When we get a girl for you, we will look for someone who doesn't read books.'

'But I'm never going to marry. It's so old fashioned, ma.' I suppressed a smile at that. Needless to say, I didn't make a case for my cousin. Even more obviously, my mother-in-law would rather he remained single than end up with a girl from my family.

This Sekar cannot just get up and leave the scene midway. He has to stay till the bitter end. There is no choice. For him, or for me.

Tuesday, 21 October 2014

I don't know how we are able to function when Sekar's undergoing chemotherapy. But like hands working involuntarily, we are making plans for a holiday. With Radha's family. We are to meet them and then go on a joint trip somewhere.

Suddenly, the holiday sounds stressful.

I don't know the protocol. I would ask Srini, but he is still moping around.

Am I on the girl's side? That would mean I will not be over-smart. I secretly wish I were on the 'boy's' side. Do these things not work like that? I ask Pari, and she simply laughs.

'Of all things, this is what you are worried about?' she says, not helping me at all. Maybe Google can.

Tuesday, 28 October 2014

Our trip is finalized now. We fly down to Philadelphia, meet Radha's folks and then drive down to more scenic places.

Radha comes by every weekend, and Pari sometimes stays over at her place. I think they don't do sleepovers here because they think we might be uncomfortable. I think we ought to feel insulted.

I've examined Pari's life this way and that, like they do diamonds at the local pawn shop, turned it around to my perspective and hers, and sought satisfactory explanations, until I figured there are none. The only thing that bothers me is that I am not all that bothered. I tried talking to Srini about it, but he seems to be on his own little trip, mostly on the information superhighway, so I let it be.

This diary will have to do. At least I have this. Srini has nothing.

Thursday, 6 November 2014

There was some talk today of visiting Niagara Falls also. I hope we don't. God, please. I don't want to go near so much water. I know She will call for me there, and I might simply follow Her. I have not told anyone about my thoughts on this, but I think Srini knows.

Thursday, 20 November 2014

It's all happening: the Winter of 2014, it's going to be called.

The kids are having a gala time, simply preparing for the trip. I am surprised they haven't been to this Philadelphia yet. And no Niagara. *Appada*!

Slowly, but surely, the focus has finally shifted from Pari and Radha to the kids. I think they're relieved too. It can be exhausting being in the spotlight. Not that I'd know.

Monday, 24 November 2014

I might not write on the road, so this might be it for a while. I'm sure I'll have a lot of things to share once I'm back. At least whatever I do remember. Some stuff evaporates so fast, like water sprinkled on a hot *dosaikkal*.

I think I should make short notes, so I can remember. I'm sure there will be tons of pictures that Srini will take. If not, there is always creativity. For if you can't remember, what's really the difference between fantasy and reality?

The girls are now calling me to shop for jeans. Me, who has only ever worn bottom-open clothes since forever? Well, once I wore a salwar kameez. I think it was the last time I was here. But jeans? I hope I don't embarrass myself too much. Maybe it's time for a new and improved version of Pankajam?

Tuesday, 25 November 2014

I must share this. Yesterday, I returned from the store, still wearing one of two jeans that the girls got me, paired with a nice olive green top, and Srini's eyes almost popped out. He's been giving me looks since then. Wonder what that's all about? I have no energy. Maybe I'll add one Calmpose to his milk at night?

We're leaving tomorrow. I'm taking my diary with me, by the way. I cannot be trusted to remember too many things. With a diary, with the words, I might be able to conjure up the memory. Even if I don't, at the very least, I have some skeleton to add flesh to.

Thursday, 27 November 2014

We were well in time for the flight. My jeans fit me perfectly, Srini had charged his phone and there was free Wi-Fi at the airport, and our bags were all checked in. I chided Pari for forcing me to wear a thick jacket. The girls (all three of them now – including Neha) had bought Srini a new jacket that he was drowning in. Srini and I even linked our arms together as we walked across to the bus that took us to the plane. It was perfect: Pari and Radha, Srini and I, and then the kids. I wished Viswa had been there but she just could not get any days off, she said.

When we landed in Philadelphia, the weather seemed pleasant enough, and I wondered what all the fuss about winter was. Of course, as soon as we stepped out, my cheeks froze. We met Radha's brother. Vikrant, he said his name was, but his friends called him Vic.

Then I wondered briefly: what about Vic and Viswa? I have become too indiscriminate, looking for opportunities anywhere and everywhere.

When we reached Radha's house, we were tired. My eyes would not stay open and the kids were fidgety. I longed for a soft bed that I could sleep in. But I knew I had to go through the rigmarole of 'meeting the parents'.

They were nice, Radha's parents. He was a finance-type guy and she a doctor. They were in clothes that matched: white shirts and jeans. I loved the way their house smelled.

'Potpourri,' Mrs Verma said, when I remarked on the fragrance in the house.

'No, thanks. We had something on the flight,' I said, and Pari laughed.

'Amma,' she said, hugging me. 'It's potpourri. It's dried flower petals that give that smell.'

The breakfast and lunch was elaborate. I told Srini if this is how regular meals are in their house, I wonder what they have at functions, but he shushed me. Srini's been acting like he's too good for me since we came here. I think he's trying to form some sort of a bond with Radha's parents; maybe trying to understand them better.

Why should he ignore me, though? I will not talk to him either.

younger kids do. I don't think I've ever hugged my parents. Or even Ammini, who was as close as anyone could get, I suppose. We held hands when we walked to school and back, and whenever we went walking, but I don't remember any hugs.

Monday, 1 December 2014

We're in Nandhimangalam all over again.

It's amazing that the one place that makes me feel like I'm back home is actually thousands of miles and three continents away from home. No TV, no internet, no cell phone. Just the village and a simple life. Lights out at dusk. Although it was super exciting when we got power for the first time, of course. The collector had to inaugurate the electricity, and there was a whole lot of brouhaha around it all. It's difficult to imagine now but all of that cheer and noise was unamplified: just people noise. The lights were all set up, but like the Krishna Jayanti *bakshanam*s, we had to wait for the collector, and he took forever to arrive. When he did, we could not wait for him to give us the electricity. Eventually it happened, and there were a lot of speeches. We later realized that electricity served the purpose of bringing more speeches to the village, not much else. However, the village finally got electricity – even if it was only a few houses that did. There were a few streetlights, but only near the village centre. Everything was a bit lopsided but still, we had lights.

Very soon, un-electrified Nandhimangalam became just a memory; I moved to electric Madras. Here, in the Amish Bed and Breakfast (it's what they give you, basically), I remember how it all was before electricity. Even if it was never so cold at home.

Thursday, 4 December 2014

The trip is done. We're on our way back.

Amish County was picturesque, for sure. To be honest I don't think I've ever been to a 'picturesque place' in my life. I mean my home town Nandhimangalam might be called picturesque by some, but somehow, to me, it just feels like home. After all, home is where you toil and sweat, suffer heartbreaks and tragedies. 'Picturesque' is a place you drive by in an AC vehicle, or alight at for a few minutes and click quick photos. It's a place where you never have to cook, where no one cares whether you have your period or not, a place where you don't have to look people in the eye. Picturesque is not a place that takes away your best friend, even as you wait for her. It's not a place that makes you wonder whether you drove her to her disappearance, and it's certainly not a place you would expect to see her even after she was gone.

Lancaster was picturesque. For once, Srini's world was not his phone. He only used it to take pictures. There were no people even if you wished for some, even if only for familiarity. There were cows grazing, chickens cluck-clucking and a couple of horses. Now all the nursery rhymes and picture books make sense. The place was a delight for everyone – other than Mr and Mrs Verma, for some reason. I got the feeling this might not be new for them. They were not very impressed with our cries of, 'Look, here's a kingfisher!' and 'Wow, a real pink pig!'

In time, I might come to think of them as *sammandhi*s. That word brings to my mind's eye a wedding and all the associated confusion. Are weddings even necessary any more, generally? I think I'd like to just have Viswa and her husband register their marriage. Even Pari and Radha. Let them walk into the sunset so I can sleep peacefully, with relatives (new and old) not squabbling about why they got the sari in a colour they already had one in, why they got the five-ringed *murukku*[7] rather than the seven-ringed one, and why they were not respected enough at the wedding.

---

7.   Fried rice snack that comes in spirals of dough, the number of rings indicating the giver's prosperity and/or the receiver's importance.

Friday, 5 December 2014

We're back home. Radha slept over the night we returned.
Not that it matters. The morning was awkward as Radha
came to the kitchen to pour herself a cup of coffee, in what
was clearly a routine action. I was seated at the counter and
when she saw me, she recoiled as if I were a snake (notice the
clever use of verbs? It's all this reading I do. Would anyone
believe it if I said I studied in Tamil medium till PUC?). Her
favourite American coffee machine lay disused and I noticed
it just then. It was filter coffee all the way since we'd arrived,
and it doubly hit home that this was the first time she had
stayed overnight since.

I wordlessly made her a cup too and we sat at the counter,
silently sipping our coffees. I had finished mine but couldn't
leave immediately. I cleared my throat.

'Nice people, your parents,' I said. Safe.

'Not really. I wish they had taken my coming out as nicely
as you guys. I can't believe you're from India. We think,
you know, Indians are, you know...'

I hadn't. I still feel it has just not sunk in. Some critical part
of my brain has not processed this. But I nodded and smiled.
The conversation might have ended there if I had not added

a little 'hmm' after that. Radha took it as encouragement to speak further.

'I knew way, way back. These things are so common here, you know.'

It seemed like I had to participate. 'We clearly had no idea, until that night,' I said truthfully.

'Yeah, I don't think Pari knew about it either for a long time.' She laughed. Her name sounded too familiar on Radha's tongue. If Srini were here, he would itch to snatch the familiarity out of it. I smiled at the thought.

'Well, anyway,' she continued, undeterred. 'When I told them – my parents – in college, they went ballistic. They threatened to kill themselves and all that crap. Can you believe it? My mom's a doctor, for God's sake!'

Radha was reliving those humiliating times. Then she seemed to brush off those memories and smiled at me.

'I'm glad we have one set of supportive parents at least,' she said.

'Hmm.'

'I know this isn't typical, but we were thinking we will get married before you guys leave.'

'Married?' My mouth must have been agape.

'Yes. Remember the proposal?'

'Ah, yes!' None of us had spoken about it, but like night follows day, wedding must follow engagement, no?

'Will a court marriage not do?' I asked.

'Yes, I guess it will.' Her face visibly shrank. If she looked into the coffee cup any longer, her face might have fallen into it.

I hit myself mentally. This was her first wedding – so what if we had been there before?

When you really think about it, no one's sexual preference should matter, except that of your significant other. The wedding would be fun – and how great would it look on my Facebook page? It would beat Padma's chatter about her Bengali son-in-law!

I reached out for her free hand and squeezed it. 'Of course, of course, we'll make it a big fat Indian wedding.'

As if on cue, Pari came walking in. Her hair looked like a cyclone had landed on her head. She gave Radha a peck. I turned away. In my defence, I would have done so even if she had given Siva a kiss. I think. Although I was never in that situation.

I must make dinner plans with Siva. Really.

Tuesday, 9 December 2014

It must be telepathy. Not with my *pati*, but with my daughter's. Ex. Soon-to-be-ex. The wordplay has lost its fun. Pun.

Basically, Siva called. Or did we call him? Anyway, we spoke. And he teased us a little bit.

'*Enna*, Aunty, you have not even called me for the past month?'

Truth be told, I'd so wanted to. I couldn't prove it unless I showed him this journal, and that was impossible. I said nothing.

'Anyway, how are you? How is Uncle?' he continued.

'We are fine, Siva. How are you?'

'Getting by.'

'We were just thinking of you and that we must surely meet,' I said.

'Sure, sure. That would be great. Say, midweek? I'll take you to dinner.'

He said he would coordinate with Pari. He called her 'Parineeta', as if he had transferred that right over to Radha. I thought I caught a hint of nostalgia.

I hung up, feeling oddly buoyant. I've stopped analysing my feelings, so I don't know why his call made me feel better. I enjoyed feeling good and that was it.

When Srini asked, 'Who was it?' I told him, and he said nothing at first. After what must have been at least five minutes, he said, 'How are we going to show him our face?' I wondered what he meant, and when my memory caught the thread of the conversation, it hit me. He still thought we were responsible for some of it. A sense of agency is healthy, but there was none here.

Srini has been very contemplative over the past month. He spent a lot of time on his phone researching this and that, but he has been less acerbic with his loose comments, so I worry for his health.

Thursday, 11 December 2014

We are back from dinner with Siva. Like little kids, we were chaperoned to the dinner and back.

Siva, ever courteous, had offered to pick us up but Pari insisted on dropping us. He had selected a nice little place, one with large windows that faced a busy street. It was on a festive main street, with little serial bulbs tied all along the way. The Christmas spirit was here in all its Coca Cola, Inc.-inspired glory, as storefronts displayed cut-out Santas of all sizes.

We could not find parking, it being the holiday and all. We called Siva, who said he was on his way. 'Call us when you are here,' Pari barked into the phone and went around in circles, looking for a spot. 'We'll just drive around till he gets here,' she said, looking straight ahead.

'Okay, ma,' Srini, who seemed to have made the passenger seat his own, said.

'Appa,' she started to say, then paused. The car suddenly grew hot.

'Appa,' she began again. 'Don't ask him too many questions.'

'Don't worry, ma,' was all he said.

'No, really. I think he still can't come to terms with it. I hear that from the kids. Don't make it worse. Don't promise things.'

'Promise what?' Srini asked. They seemed to have shut me out of the conversation and I wanted to care less.

'You know, that this is a fad or something. I know you can't understand it yet, but it's real, Appa.'

Srini was silent. I piped up, 'Don't worry, Pari. We just want to meet him for a nice dinner and be pleasant.'

She looked at me sharply.

'Amma,' she said loudly. 'Sometimes I wonder if your mind has even processed this.'

'What?'

'You think everything is a joke. An experience for *you*. So now, it's about *you* having a gay daughter. How could you possibly be cool about it? Accepting, yes, but so cool about it? Like, no questions asked? Don't you even wonder, when did I first know? When did I first suspect? How I met Radha? How difficult it was to find out, to come out, to tell

71

Siva, to tell my kids? Did you ever wonder? Maybe even, I don't know, how we do *it*? Appa at least has these questions and I can see that he's struggling with all of it. He's trying to understand. You, Amma, I wish I could say the same.'

When did it become about me? And Srini had been asking her questions without discussing them with me? I felt my head spinning. Perhaps, I thought, Pari was right.

I did not speak.

Srini, the traitor, was explaining to Pari: 'Pari, Amma deals with things differently. Not everyone is the same.'

I saw Pari's eyes film over in the rear-view mirror. I wanted to reach out to her and say, 'There, there,' or something equally appropriate, but Srini beat me to it, placed his hand on her right hand, which was on the gear box, and squeezed it. She looked up at him gratefully.

I could not wait to meet Siva.

When Siva finally made it, he called us and then stood by the edge of the car. Instead of opening my car door, he went up to Pari's window and whispered something to her. She nodded and we all alighted.

Pari zoomed off without even looking back and Siva gave Srini's hand a shake. He gave me a staid namaste and then, laughing, hugged me sideways, my shoulders easily fitting into his long arms. I smelled a strong perfume envelope me, as he squeezed my shoulder and let it go. I remember, even now, how we had monitored his arm length, me declaring that his long arms meant that he was an artist by temperament. And how my niece had warned Pari, to ensure that he was, in fact, interested in women. How we all thought it was very funny at the time.

He led the way in, stated, 'Three for Venugopal,' to the smartly dressed woman, and entered the dining area. A waiter helped us to our table and he pulled out a chair for me and Srini too. As soon we were settled a waiter hovered and Siva gestured to him. He then looked at us and smiled. 'I'm not sure we're celebrating anything,' he said, 'but what the hell!'

Srini gave a sad smile as the waiter offered Siva the wine menu. He looked it over, selected something I hadn't heard of before, and said, 'A bottle.' I nearly whistled. That was bound to be expensive.

'Relax, Aunty,' he said. 'Don't worry. It's not every day that I get to treat my parents-in-law.'

'Ex,' he added.

'That is true,' I said, and looked straight at him. I wanted to ask him so many things, tell him a lot too. I didn't know what he wanted to hear. I simply said, 'We are so sorry,' and looked at Srini, who nodded and added, 'We had no idea.'

'Well, Aunty,' Siva said. 'I can't say it was a big shock, obviously.' He laughed. 'There are only so many headaches that can make sense.'

'How are you, Siva?' I asked and he replied, standardly, 'Good, thanks.' The stock reply in the tone I had heard people say it, in parks, in check-out counters, everywhere.

'Really, how are you holding up?' I persisted.

'Really, I'm fine. I think people expect me to be sad, devastated, and it's been a shock, sure, but you move on.'

'Like a death of a loved one,' Srini said, totally inappropriately.

He talked about this and that, and a little bit about his business. I ordered a salad, Srini ordered an aubergine lasagne and Siva ordered a steak.

'I didn't know you ate beef.' The words escaped my mouth before I realized what I had said. He had never touched beef in all the years I knew him, and he always celebrated all the festivals diligently and all of that, so you know, it was a bit of a shock.

'Really?' Siva said. 'My beef eating? That's what's remarkable about this situation?' I thought I detected an angry tone, but I suppose he was entitled to that. And then he laughed. It was one of those inverted pyramid laughs, with each layer building up on the one below it, growing in pitch and intensity. We waited for it to end and he started, 'Sorry, sorry, but that was just too funny.'

I swallowed, but the food wouldn't go down easily. The rest of the meal proceeded in relative silence, if we discounted Srini's grunting as he wolfed down his lasagne.

He told us about his parents, how they didn't know anything, and if we could, please, not tell them yet. They had also wondered, like us, how they never spoke with Pari whenever he called them.

'When are you going to tell them?' I asked. 'You might be surprised. I never thought I would be okay with it all. Never thought I would be planning a lesbian wedding!'

Siva's eyes narrowed. 'They are getting married?'

'Um,' I stalled. 'There's talk, of course.'

'Really?' His face cleared. 'Oh, well. I guess it was inevitable.'

I told him he must also find someone else. After all, he wasn't that old.

'It doesn't matter if you're old here, Aunty,' he said. 'You just tell me if you're bored of Uncle.'

Srini laughed again and just like that the cloud had passed, without us getting drenched in the downpour. I don't remember a lot of what we spoke about after that, but I remember feeling all warm and fuzzy.

I would not divulge this to anyone else, not even Srini, but a fleeting thought just entered my mind: how about Viswa and Siva? I think these medicines are messing me up.

Monday, 15 December 2014

Not much to report. Everything is as usual, sort of.

The kids have begun to really warm up to me and I'm happy about that. They really want to play with me and talk to me and do all that grandmotherly stuff with me.

Something about it, though, seems forced. I never was much of a child person, so I guess I'm finding it difficult. I'll say it on behalf of all the grandmothers who never felt it: not all grandmothers can play with kids for hours. Some of us are different. While we're at it, this too: not all of us are happy about being babysitters; your kids' poop is not brown gold; and your life decisions should not automatically take precedence over mine. There. Done!

On another note, Pari and Radha got a Christmas tree today. It is a beautiful one, and really alive.

In Chennai, our neighbour used to keep a tree, but you could smell the plastic from a mile away. At least, what I now know as plastic mixed with artificial Christmas tree scent they put on the tree. Mrs Xavier, she was, and quite nice too. She gave us all cookies and cake for Christmas. Xavier – her husband, that is – had left her, but she remained Mrs Xavier to us. We never thought of it then, how bad she must have felt that she was constantly reminded of the runaway husband. In fact, I don't know her name; not sure if I ever did.

Xavier – the only name Pari and Viswa knew that started with an 'X'. They used it to death whenever they played

Name, Place, Animal, Thing. That is, until one of them insisted there was a name called Xuma, and after that it was always a toss-up between the two. It became interesting because with just Xavier, they were sure they would each get five points, but with two options, it became a gamble. Until they decided to split up the names. Pari (I think) would always use Xavier and Viswa, always Xuma. That's when I joined the game and messed up their planned life. They wouldn't know which I would use and so they wouldn't stick to the script either. It was fun watching them try to second guess me.

Saturday, 20 December 2014

I'm off to sleep now but I have to write that I am totally in love with Christmas. The love, the joy, the spirit of it all! I think the girls got me a little drunk tonight. I kissed everyone, I think. I did a lot of things that I don't usually, and I imagine that others did too.

I asked Pari if the Coke had something in it, but she denied it. It tasted funny though. But then, I've been battling a cold and everything tastes different. We had music and the kids were there for a bit before being banished upstairs. I noticed their eyes for the first time today. Clear and a dark shade of brown, identical but different in size, like stacked cups. Shaped like almonds. Curious, bright, full of life. And love. I sat in a corner and watched them as the first song of the evening was played by Radha, the resident DJ. The kids were looking at Pari and Radha dancing away and they laughed. Neha tugged at Radha's dupatta and she lifted the kid up and danced with her too. Pari grabbed Neel's hand and they danced away, starting with what seemed like practised moves and ending with what I can only categorize as random *saami aadal*. No one in that room was any good, I thought, before a wave of shame washed over me. It wasn't about how good you looked to others; it was about how good you felt inside. Even Srini was moving about in the corner by the lamp, as Pari dragged him to the centre of the room and he begged off, laughing. Then Neel took over, his limbs with a mind of their own. His dancing was like the spin cycle of the washing machine; everyone but Neha moved to the sides of the room. It was amazing, this Christmas. There was a wine bottle on the table, courtesy Siva. 'Merry Christmas to Radha and Pari. Here's to many more!' he had written on the card that was tied to it in a neat bow. Even my cynical mind could not stop warmth from spreading across my chest like ink on blotting paper.

I love this festival. I love my family. And yes, Radha is part of it. Oh, and my grandkids are the loveliest in the world. And I love them too.

I would pick their brown gold poop in an...well, I'm not that intoxicated.

Good night and Merry Christmas!

Thursday, 1 January 2015

Happy New Year!

Feels a bit weird to write that. It's not as if fortunes are like targeted injections — they are slow, meandering things that take ages to form, each breath building on the earlier one. I suppose I could wish that we keep taking those breaths. It feels a bit low-key, this New Year's. I made payasam anyway.

L&T South City, Bengaluru

Monday, 5 January 2015

This is going to be the year of weddings in our family, I think.

Viswa, Prathik and maybe even my brother's son from Delhi! And, I'm guessing, Pari. It's going to be difficult to top Pari's for shock and entertainment value.

It's good to be back in India. It's like I'm swimming with the flow, and not against it. I wish we were back in Chennai though. Viswa's called us over and so here we are – I suppose we don't have a choice, at least for a month.

It's a nice place, it is. And so many of us Tamil people, so it almost feels like Bella. Except for the ladies. I am forever asking people here their names, and I expect they are tired of telling me. I can't wait for the next edition of the Bella Bhakti Group. They welcomed me back but, shockingly, no one has asked me about Pari. Isn't that weird?

Monday, 12 January 2015

Bhogi's coming, and so I need to get ready. I keep saying it doesn't make sense here, high up here, in Bengaluru to boot. It feels like a *pottu* and jeans combination. In fact, Pongal stopped being relevant for me when I got married and came to Madras. Back home, it was *the* festival. It was as if the whole village had an oil bath and got decked up for a wedding – flowers everywhere, children playing, and cattle's horns painted in bright colours. It was the climax of all the activity over the past two months. The sacks of paddy were either ready to be sent or would already have been sent. Schools rarely functioned in January. If they did, they were poorly attended.

For as long as I can remember, we made *koottu* pongal. All the ladies came outside their own houses and made pongal. There were other streets and other pongals too. The ululation of the women as the pongal boiled over was only matched by the fervour of us kids shouting, '*Pongalo pongal*,' '*Pongalo pongal*.'

Ammini and I were the first to all these celebrations. We would hang out everywhere: by the ladies, by the cows and bulls, and watch longingly as the young men would get ready

81

for the highlight at the end of the festival: *Jallikattu*. Man against bull. Sometimes, there was so much silence, especially just before the bull would charge, that even its snort would be heard. '*Fusssss.*' For the longest time, Ammini wanted to be in the *jallikattu*. She even told the teacher who asked her what she wanted to be when she grew up: I want to be in the *jallikattu*. A lot of ridicule piled up on her and so I had to step in and say I wanted to be one too. (Everyone knew there was no way I would enter the ground ever.) It turned out that my standing up for her, of sorts, didn't really help, and we were both then teased.

The Pongal after that declaration in class, I nearly always kept her in my eyesight, lest Ammini jump over the hastily-constructed fence, in an attempt to become the first-ever woman *jallikattu veeranganai*.[8] That didn't happen, obviously, but she was fuming, as I put it, 'much like the bull itself'.

The year after she went away, on Pongal, I found myself frozen. The '*pongalo pongal*' was stuck in my throat, even as I could feel it bubble up. I tried dislodging it but all that came out were tears. It was impossible for me to say anything and during the *jallikattu* I found myself cheering for the bulls.

8. Female version of hero. Not to be confused with heroine, who, most of the time, needs rescuing.

Since then itself, actually, Pongal has lost its sheen. It wasn't after I got married, I suppose. It was after she went away.

Tuesday, 20 January 2015

Pongal has meant one thing: *thai maasam*. The harbinger of good fortune. After the Dakshinayanam, when Gods are worshipped and focused on, it is time for people to take care of themselves. That means reopening Viswa's matrimonial prospects et al. I feel good about this year. Pari has not told us anything but I am guessing that the engagement will soon fructify into a wedding. As if everything is just the same – only a person (and gender) has changed. Is it really that easy? I don't know. Maybe they'll even have a honeymoon? God knows.

I remember ours – it was to Ernakulam, and from there, to Alappuzha. It had just started, this idea of a honeymoon, in those days. We sat in the back of a friend's car with the driver in the front seat. Our hands were touching under my shawl. Srini's hands made their way up mine, even as he carried on a conversation with the driver about the upcoming Cricket World Cup – the first ever. They talked incessantly about the entire line-up, and the prospects of this player and that, and in particular one Abid Ali. Srini apparently felt that Abid was not given the importance he deserved. I tried to concentrate but failed miserably since Srini's palm started kneading my waist as if that would make it any softer.

Privacy was so coveted and seemingly illegal, like stolen mangoes from a neighbour's garden, that when we were finally by ourselves in a riverboat, we barely touched.

As a side effect of that car ride, though, Abid Ali, the unlucky cricketer, appeared in my dreams for months afterwards. Even years later, like even now, I could tell you about him, even as the world has likely forgotten him: a player from Hyderabad, who was underutilized. He had to play second fiddle to the spin quartet who ruled Indian cricket then. If he were alive today he would have done an amazing job in T20 cricket – Srini told me just the other day – so fit was he. The biggest side effect is that even today, when anyone says the word 'honeymoon', Abid Ali and the car ride come to mind.

Monday, 26 January 2015

I remember the parade we watched on TV today. Forget people marching in order, there were camels matching steps! We (that's Srini and me, Viswa was still sleeping in) watched it on one of those new channels first, but then there was so much text going up and down, left and right, that it started to do something in my head.

I asked Srini to change it to good old Doordarshan. I was surprised DD also had all kinds of text on the screen, but it was doddering along like me, not zooming around like a teenager. The commentary was in Hindi and that put Srini off, but I was okay with watching it on mute also. After all, it was the same old thing every year.

'And here, you have the wonderful culture of (whatever state) being represented in all its glory... What a sight it is to see this colourful tableau representing this great country...'

Sometime in between, Sekar called to wish us a happy Republic Day. Who wishes someone on 26 January? I think he just wanted to talk to us. It was good to hear his voice. He was sounding much better, and said he was feeling better too. I wanted to go home soon, home to Palm Bella Vista, and I hope that will be sooner rather than later.

Srini seemed oddly excited about the chief guest. I didn't even know this thing had chief guests. He thinks it's a strategic move – for him everything is strategic, even my menu of the day (which, like this diary, is usually random). The chief guest is the POTUS, as the television kept reminding me. If we had the acronym in India, it would be POI (does not translate well, though – *poi* is untruth in Tamil).

When our school had a chief guest, it was almost always an old man who could not speak faster than five words a minute. We waited, fidgeted, and would finally start clapping midway only to receive murderous stares from the teachers. One year, they asked me to speak at the parade at school. It was on the importance of the national flag. The teachers wrote it all down for me, and made me practise a thousand times, after, before and during school. Like I couldn't handle one minute of talking. But on the day of the speech, of course, I faltered. I stuttered and stammered but finally got to the end of it.

The speech was over, but a fight with Ammini started. She didn't speak with me for four whole months. She had wanted to be the speaker. If only she had told me, I would have gladly given it up. She didn't speak to me until the summer holidays and by then I guess we were too bored to be mad at each other.

When she was gone, I often thought of those four months, February to June, when I didn't speak with her. During those four months I played back our old conversations in my head, so I didn't even miss her all that much. She was irritated that I wasn't desperate to speak with her – 'Are you made of stone, *di*?' – while she couldn't resist speaking with me. 'You need more imagination, *di*,' I said. She would have gone another four months without talking, if only she could bear it.

After she disappeared, I would often wonder if I could trick my mind into thinking that she was still here in our village; only I couldn't talk to her? It wasn't easy. The brain intervened. Those four months were not easy to recreate after she went away.

The mangoes in Ammini's *thoppu* were extra sweet the year of The Fight. You know the sweetness that travels from your tongue all the way down to your throat, and seems to dissipate to all parts of your body, as if it were angiogram dye? We hardly get mangoes like that now. They're all big, fat, cheap Banganapallis and somehow even the sweetness seems medicinal – perhaps because of all the chemicals that artificially ripen the mangoes. Nothing that's artificial can touch your soul – be it mangoes, or relationships. There! That's my philosophical statement of the day.

Saturday, 7 February 2015

The past week has been a blur. There was a 'boy-seeing' in the house, although Viswa would have cringed at the semantics of it. There was to be no 'seeing', by strict instructions. In fact, she did not even want the boy's parents to come.

As a consequence, the boy-seeing happened with minimal fuss. We did not even have to ask them to go speak with each other. Viswa just beckoned him and led him to the bedroom. There was no clearing of the throat and our magnanimous utterance, prefaced by a fake laugh, 'What interest will the young kids have in our old people talk? Let them go speak. This is the fashion these days,' or some such, followed by my showing them to an appropriate room. None of that. They just got up, even as we were to get into our own conversation, tracing our families across generations, looking for a connection somewhere, like looking for the source of ant lines. They closed the door, and we opened our mouths. As the boy's parents looked on at me incredulously, likely fazed by the gumption of the girl, I simply ignored them and continued talking about the latest issue of *Kalki* magazine, where a new series by a film director had made its debut. All eyes reverted to the locked door, and I knew they were all making a big deal out of nothing. Isn't it good to have a strong female in the house? Wasn't *shakti* the word for power, strength, the female deity? Srini was already hidden behind his Android screen, thumbing the screen up and down, as if he had nothing to do with this family.

When *Kalki*'s new series did not catch anyone's fancy, I tried another tack: *Amma*. Surely, everyone knows her? If not, just search 'Amma TN' on Google. That topic might have been a slippery slope, but at least it would keep people from overusing their imagination.

'So what about Amma's case, huh?' I began, knowing we would somehow find common ground. 'What will happen? You think Karnataka High Court will find her guilty?'

That seemed to catch the attention of the boy's father. He had retired from service in the state government and in the manner of public servants assumed an air of superior knowledge about the inner workings of the government, as if there was a secret tunnel system of government offices across the country rivalling London's subway.

'What do you mean?' he asked sharply, peeling his eyes away from the door and fixing them on my face.

'Well, you know, it's been in the news all over... Surely, she will not let it be? She will make sure the Karnataka High Court acquit her, no?'

'What do you mean?' His voice was belligerent, and it seemed like he was not used to his opinion being questioned, by a woman, no less. I could see his nostril hair swaying dangerously like coconut trees in a cyclone.

Never mind that the person we were talking about, one of the most powerful politicians in the country, was also a woman. What is it about power that renders a woman genderless?

'Amma. Jayalalithaa. Surely, you've been following the news?'

'Yes, yes, of course. What do you mean? Do you mean she should go to jail?'

His voice had risen by several decibels, as he thundered with all his might. I desperately looked at Srini, who had turned temporarily deaf. I desperately looked at the closed door, hoping the couple would emerge, but no such luck.

'Yes, ma'am. Maybe you can explain what you said? That she will bribe someone and come out?'

I remained silent. He seemed too invested in it – no sense in rattling that cage.

'Even if it is true, so what? Millions of Tamilians have reposed faith in her. Then, what can the problem be?'

I said nothing, in a way that made it clear I did not agree. I had no wish to be dragged into a debate. I just wanted for the kids to come out of the room.

'What are you saying? You think you know more than everyone else? Who has given you the right?' he shouted.

I would have thrown something at him if he had not been a prospective *sammandhi*, the likelihood of which was decreasing by the minute. Maybe the young lovebirds should not have left *us* alone. His wife seemed immune to his raised voice and quivering nostrils, doubtless having borne the brunt of several such outbursts. She was examining the *vadai*[9] and signalled to a distraught me that it was indeed very good.

I wondered whether I should allow my daughter to be married into such a patriarchal family. They likely wondered whether their son should be married into such a matriarchal one. God knows. All further discussion was stopped by the unbolting of the door.

9. The fried snack with the hole.

The room heaved a collective sigh of relief; only Mr Quivering Nostrils seemed a bit disappointed at having lost the opportunity to put me down. The two of them, Viswa and Sonu, emerged, smiling, and that was always a good sign. After a bit of sundry chat, they left. Viswa went straight back to her room but before she could bolt it, I put my foot in the door.

'*Enna aachu, di*? What's the verdict?' I asked.

'What?' She had the gall to sound exasperated and roll her eyes. We had searched for a boy for her, a boy she seemed to like. I'd have liked to see her say thanks, at the very least.

'So? How did it go?'

'It was all right. He seems like a nice guy.'

'Is that a yes, then?'

'What? How can I make a choice in fifteen minutes, Amma? We've decided to talk more.'

Talk more. Two words that could spell trouble for any budding relationship. If it involved my dear younger daughter, destruction of aforementioned relationship was guaranteed.

'Talk *more*? But why?'

'I can't know anything about him in such a short time, Ma. I know more about my company watchman than I do about him.' I briefly wondered about the marital status of the said watchman before asking: 'How long do you think you'll need to do this...this talking?'

She just shook her head as if I was a dumb creature. 'Till I get to his soul. *Podhuma?*'

'Soul? What kind of nonsense is that? Are you Satan or what? Why do you need to get to his soul?' I mumbled, and turned around.

'Amma, wait,' Viswa called out. She must have felt the need to explain things to me. 'See, Ma, it's like the water from a pump. The first few mugs are useless, tainted, muddied. So it is with him and me, I'm sure. I've told him I love watching documentaries, that I love the theatre and that I am slightly religious. These are all things that are, let's just say, curated truths. But you see, it's to make him think I'm better than I am. I'm sure he's told me a bunch of half-truths too. We have to wait for a few more meetings for us to know each other. The way he negotiates a roadside beggar, the way he treats the coffee shop waiter and the way he deals with traffic, all of that will tell me more about him, and him more about me. It is in these unguarded moments that we are likely to fall in, or out of, love.'

I was amazed. Why hasn't anyone lapped her up yet?

Since then, it's been a week of them chatting and meeting and doing God-knows-what.

In the meantime, we're just waiting, two accused waiting for the jury to reach a verdict.

Thursday, 19 February 2015

That boy will, apparently, 'not work out'. The son of Mr Quivering Nostrils.

I don't want to even ask her why. She had refused parallel processing of prospective grooms, pushing me back to square one. It must be something to do with Valentine's Day. Why did it have to come right in between their budding romance?

I can't for the life of me think what the objection to a love marriage could ever have been. I dare not say this to Viswa, but look at Pari – she's gone and found herself someone. I don't even know where they met, how they got to know each other.

This looking, matching and setting up only to be summarily rejected is too much trouble. There is no choice, though, is there? Surely, there are young men in her office? I'd asked her way back, and she said there is no one and added that I need not do this looking if I don't want to. So I'm just going to have to trudge on. In a moment of unbridled optimism, I've gone and forgotten the TamilMatrimony.com password.

Friday, 20 February 2015

I got the password and also a bunch of prospects. Srini told me there is a sales software that we can use for our search. He and his comedy. I was surprised to see Vasu's son is on the site too. He's a good kid. Maybe I can informally introduce the two of them and see where it goes?

Srini, as always, has left all of this to me. He says he would sign the cheques when it comes to it. We have a joint account, so I'm not exactly sure how that's helping anything we're doing. I want to grab his phone and throw it off our balcony.

Saturday, 28 February 2015

We have to go back to the US. Pari is getting married.

We were just there and I don't feel like the twenty-four-hour flight. But I have no choice. How can I not go to my own daughter's wedding? Viswa tells us she will come later.

I really wish the wedding were next year or something.

I feel too tired. I can't take another change of place. My heart's in Nandhimangalam, my muscle memory in Chennai, my memories all over, and my body cannot, just cannot, be somewhere else.

The United States of America

Saturday, 7 March 2015

There are parts of Pari's house that I like. Mostly because I remember my way around them. The kitchen is large, wide open, with an island, which is where I like to sit. The front yard is pretty also, even if the plants have withered. I assume Siva used to take care of them. Pari tries very hard to remember to water them, to care for them, but I've learned the hard way that plants are not like kids; it's not enough if you simply feed them.

Everyone assumes that people from the village know all about gardens and plants, but the truth is we only know about the crops that we grow. If that. When I came to Madras after the wedding, people used to ask me about their gardens. 'How often I should water a rose plant?' kind of questions. I had no idea. The first time I saw a rose plant was in the city anyway.

Funnily, I'd never thought of our Nandhimangalam house as a house, the way I think of Pari's, or even our Bella Vista apartment. When I came to Srini's house after the wedding, I saw the rooms as rooms. It was really the first time I thought of a building as a home. Nandhimangalam, like Amma's breasts, simply nurtured me, and I have no memory of how it looked.

One summer, we went on a temple trip, the one parents usually take when they realize their children are not like them; diagnosing a lack of culture and values, they embark on these trips, as if culture lay in temples and grandiose structures, and not in themselves. That summer, we mixed Gangaikonda Cholapuram with Chidambaram, eager to showcase the endurance of our culture, both architectural and religious. In the car, Srini and Sekar took turns telling the bored children the wonders of the temples and their uniqueness ('Do you know the Chidambaram Deekshitars were appointed by Sivaperuman to take care of his worship?'). I said I wanted to visit my village and the brothers agreed. Renuka was fiddling in the bag to feed the children something.

The road that led from the main road to our village looked different. It had been so many years, too many to keep count. We entered the dusty road and then the village, even as bored middle-aged men stood around, peering into the car at the seemingly lost people.

I rolled down the windows to smell the village, to remember, and immediately, complaints ensued. Dirt. Heat.

Smell. Everything I was, was a problem to the children. Somehow we located our old house, or what stood in place of it: a garish orange and green imposter. I walked up and down, over to where Ammini's house once (and amazingly, still) was. Just as it had stood all those years ago, it waited for the girl of the house to return, only it was hollowed out, like an autopsied cadaver. The family, I knew, had left for Delhi, to be with her brother who had joined the army. I went closer, pushing my way through the underbrush typical of a dilapidated house. Creepers had claimed the walls, and plants and trees peeked out of windows and doors. Unmindful of the scratches and the stares I walked on through the front door, half expecting to see Ammini sitting by her favourite wall, waiting for me.

Instead, I saw more signs of decay – the bricks were visible in most places and the moss nearly tripped me up. 'Ammini,' I cried out several times, only stopping when I heard a sound behind me. I turned – had she heard me? Had she been waiting? Why did I take so long to return? – and saw Srini (or maybe it was Sekar). I fell to my knees, sobbing. I vowed never to visit the village again. She wasn't here, but meet her I would, of this I was sure.

Saturday, 14 March 2015

Everything is about the wedding now. THE wedding. It's just a little over a month away.

I can't help but think of this second wedding, while Viswa's not even had her first (and only, and only). In our day, the order of weddings was sacrosanct. You couldn't alter it as you pleased. The girls were first to be married, unless a brother was much older than the next eligible sister. (Caveat: If there were several sisters, brothers could get married earlier, so that money could be prepared for the sisters' weddings.)

For example, if there was a twenty-two-year-old girl and a twenty-six-year-old brother, woe betide the brother who got married before the sister, before sincere and reasonable efforts were made to get the sister married. So many brothers remain lifelong bachelors because their sisters are not married on time, or worse, married late. Ones that did go ahead and get married were selfish for jumping the invisible queue. Parents were supposed to frown on it and be a bit angry about it, no matter how they really felt.

Through most of the planning, I am a keen listener but a reluctant participant. I feel a bit removed. Like how we Tamils feel about Kashmir. We know we must be bothered about it and have an opinion, but truth be told, most of us don't care all that much.

Spring, Radha and Pari seem to think, was the best time as it was the season for new blooms. I suppose winter, in contrast, would be the time to die, if there was ever a good time for it.

The wedding is here, in SFO ('*Paati*, no one says San Francisco. Say SFO, or SanFran.'). I suppose that means we are the girl's side. Srini tells me I am giving too much importance to this – who is what in this situation – and perhaps he is right.

They actually have wedding planners for same-sex couples here! But Radha and Pari, Indian blood as they have, have decided to do it all themselves ('Those guys charge a bomb, Pa,' they said. Radha has taken to calling us Pa and Ma. I don't mind, but there is no need.). I offered to do anything to help, and they said they would ask me if it came to it, and that was that.

We'll return home to India after the wedding, before they leave for their honeymoon.

Saturday, 21 March 2015

The priests came home. I didn't understand who they were at first. They wore shirts and pants like anyone else, and even had a jacket on. They didn't even have *vibhuti* on. There was a faint memory of it on their foreheads, like the Indian accent in Pari's English.

I had only seen bare-bodied priests and thought they were kidding when they introduced themselves. I thought they were Radha and Pari's friends. Only after they started talking about the ceremony did I realize who they were.

They settled down on the sofas and I offered them some coffee, and we began the discussion. That is, they told us what they had already done before for many couples.

'We can go with an English version or a Sanskrit one, or you can write your own as well.'

'One couple did a beautiful hybrid ceremony: they put their rings in the *homam* fire and retrieved them at the end of the ceremony, putting it on each other at the reception.'

'We have also done a wedding where everything was completely traditional. Absolutely no change, only we replaced the pronouns.'

It was then that it hit me, with the priests in the shirts and pants and jackets, with Srini deliberating the discussions: it was all nonsense. Why were we even doing the traditional thing when our situation was as non-traditional as it could get?

I remember my wedding, Srini and I not understanding even a bit of the rituals and just going along with it simply to get to the end of it, like reading a badly written murder mystery.

This more thoughtful, more involved ritual was disconcerting, and I realized I had problems with it. I did not see the need for it. It was like trying to use a small mixie jar for making idli *maavu*. It was the wrong tool. No ceremony was required for love. Weddings were different, weren't they? They were the honouring of a social contract. This was a declaration of love. This was not that.

My head began to pound.

Turning to Srini, I said, 'Sorry,' and climbed the stairs to our room, where I hoped to lie down and calm a raging headache.

Srini just gave me a piece of his mind. He came to the room after the priests had left and shook my sleep-acting self.

'What was that nonsense?' he asked.

'What nonsense?'

'You know what I am talking about!'

It is very difficult to live with a heart patient who you want to fight with. You can't talk back; you can't do anything shocking (although Pari seemed to have done a pretty good job); and you certainly cannot escalate the situation. The fear, instilled by years of Tamil movies, is real; whether it is justified or not is another matter. I just kept quiet, although every nerve in my throat was fighting for an outlet.

'It's not easy for anyone,' he continued. 'And you were the one who embraced her new life wholeheartedly. What has happened to you?'

I felt myself blinking rapidly. 'I don't know. I'm okay with it, and I'm living with it. But why marry? And if they must, why must they marry with priests and all? What is even the need? Why can't they just live like they are doing now?'

I suppose I believe that if all of this is done under the radar, we may escape the wrath of the Gods. Having a proper ceremony involving Gods is sort of like pressing that button to call the air hostess. It lights up some corresponding bulb up there, and the Gods are notified. Then your case is taken up for scrutiny.

I mean, that's how I see it. I've not been too religious for the same reason.

Srini walked away in a huff, and I felt suitably chastised. Perhaps I was making too much of it all. It really didn't matter, did it?

Perhaps things are different now and marriages can only be about love, and what follows. I knew love when I saw it. Pari and Radha, yes, double yes.

Monday, 23 March 2015

Sekar is not coming for the wedding. It was obvious, Srini said, but I had had hope. He seemed very stressed though. When we left, his treatment was coming along well. When

103

we visited him before coming here, he was nothing like the ~~boy~~ man I knew, but Renuka said he had improved greatly. Thank God we hadn't made video calls from America when he was in bad shape.

That day, after lunch – a usual sumptuous spread by Renuka (most of which Sekar could not eat, and I felt bad for him) – Srini and Sekar settled in the hall to speak about the doctors and hospitals and how everyone was only out to get money. Renuka and I retreated to the kitchen to clear up.

'Our medicine has everything, you know. There is nothing that Ayurveda cannot cure,' I heard Sekar say. I panicked. I hoped he wouldn't cut off his allopathy treatment. But one look at Renuka, as the two brothers discussed the wonders of natural and ancient medicine, and I realized she wouldn't let him do anything silly.

'Look at them talk,' she said as we stood in the kitchen. I was distinctly reminded of the Vandalur Zoo. 'All they do is talk. Can anything be achieved by thinking and talking? You need action, action.'

It felt like a barb.

Renuka continued, 'Everyone thinks I don't know much, simply because I don't talk much.'

My stomach did something funny. I mumbled something and walked to the hall where the two brothers were discussing Sekar's cancer, as if it were nothing but the latest T20 score.

'Doctor has given me a lot of hope, *da*,' Sekar said, as I sat down. 'He said we caught it early. Stopped it from spreading at the right time. Stopped it from taking over the whole body.' Sekar looked at me as he said this. My stomach was still feeling odd. I wanted to get up, but couldn't.

'That's great. Modern medicine...' I began, but stopped short. That was what began this conversation in the first place. Everyone was upbeat when we left, and I supposed I'd extrapolated it to mean that everything will be back to normal by the time Pari's wedding came along.

He was getting better, and would become all right soon, the doctors had said, but travel was out of the question.

'Let Prathik take a week off and come for the wedding,' I said one day.

We chat nearly every day on WhatsApp. I save all chats, but maybe I should start deleting them. That makes all the apps slow, I'm told. But I'm finding it more and more difficult to let things go now, for they are the *thorattis*[10] that are letting me access those hard-to-reach memories. This is what Sekar and I chatted about after I asked him whether he will come for the wedding.

Manni, you are crazy. I'm having all this chemo and all you can think about is your daughter's wedding?

10. Fruit picker; to pick from the tree, not the bowl.

No, no, Sekar. It will be a good break.

For whom?

Prathik. And you. You must be feeling guilty that your son is going hospital to hospital with you.

Well, no. That's his duty.

I know you, Sekar. You must be feeling bad. When does he need to be there?

The sessions are happening now. After a month, we will know whether they are working.

Of course they will. Then what happens?

Then, they will decrease the frequency and then test again.

Let me ask you something.

Can Renuka not accompany you to the sessions?

Really, manni, you are the limit. That's actually none of your business. Must I tell you? We are not in a position to spend lakhs on a trip for the second marriage of your daughter. Marriage to another woman, no less.

Hmm... That actually makes sense. Do you need any money, then? Or we can sponsor Prathik's trip here.

Both are the same, no?

Thanks, manni. I really did not mean to insult Pari.

But where did you? It is her second marriage only.

Yeah, that is true. I am so glad there is someone I can vent to. To be mean to.

Yes, of course. I hope you will return the favour someday.

BTW, do you know that priests here have refined marriage manthirams for people like Pari?

What?

Like they have filtered out some of the manthirams, based on the meaning, to create a special ceremony for girl–girl, man–man weddings.

Ah! Can I ask you something, manni?

Of course.

Are you really okay with this? What do you really think? How was it when she first told you?

I think I forgot.

But Pari is angry that I was okay with it too soon. I guess, like you, she accused me of thinking only about myself. Maybe she's right. Maybe I haven't explored it properly.

Then the screen just said, *Typing, typing, typing…* for a long time, and then there was no message from him. Maybe the internet had disconnected. That happens a lot back home. When it does, we walk up to the modem, switch it off and turn it back on. Srini and I fight for whose turn it is to go do that.

Oh, and Tamil New Year is around the corner.

Neha asked me why we have a different new year, and I told her it was all about new beginnings.

'Why is English New Year 1st January?' I asked her in return.

'Because that's real new year!' she answered with the confidence of a child.

'Shouldn't the new year bring at least a new season? In India, as it is here, spring is when the old gives way to the new, so it's in sync with nature.'

I'm not exactly sure what she understood, but she said, 'Uh-huh,' the way Americans do, and proceeded to dip her finger in the mango *pachadi* I had made for her. We then watched something on YouTube about the festival. It was a lot of fun. She calls me Panku Paati and that is the sweetest nickname ever. Neel is a bit more reserved. He liked the *manga pachadi* too. I am shocked they have not tasted it before. What is this girl Parineeta doing? It seems like they might go to Siva's house for the weekend. I don't want to let them go. These bonds are new, and I'm scared. I won't want to be sucked into a new whirlpool of feelings that I can't handle, manage, reciprocate appropriately and, worst of all, remember.

Saturday, 28 March 2015

When I was a new bride, I never had any expectations. I never even wanted my mother-in-law to like me or anything. That's a big deal when you enter a house as a new bride, you know — do you get along with your mother-in-law?

We weren't so bad, my mother-in-law and I. There were niggling issues, as is certain with any girl who thinks independently, I imagine. It's just the way things are. Our relationship was more like hot water on the stove, roiling around within the vessel, but never in danger of boiling over, or spoiling like milk.

I want to say it's because Srini handled it well, but I know in my heart that it was Sekar. He was the apple of her eye and he always took my side so she simply had to follow suit. She left us soon enough though. A month or so bedridden, if that, and then just gone. His father had expired a long time ago. That's a funny word: expired. When I was young, 'expired' was a serious word used for dying. And only humans. These days, when someone says 'expired', you think of packaged foods, or medicines, or shopkeepers who stock old stuff. For dying, people just say the word, as if it does not even warrant euphemism.

Sunday, 29 March 2015

I forgot to complete what I started yesterday, so let me get to it right away. Sometimes, really, it's easier to create memories than to recall them. It seems I went walking and forgot the way home. Pari and Srini are worried and want to take me to the doctor right away. But I think it's because the houses are all the same. Back home, it was easy to remember: left at the bright green house and then right near the dustbin until you reach the construction site (which will change to 'the building with rubble in front', to 'new building', to whatever). How do I remember things here? Right at the grey house, next to the grey house and then take a left at the grey house? And I don't even know the trees here to remember them by their names. I'm assuming there's a lot of oak, walnut and spruce, because these are all street names in nearly every town.

Still, they are scared. So I can only go out supervised. And I hear even Neel is acceptable as a supervisor. Oh, well.

Wednesday, 1 April 2015

You will not believe what happened yesterday. We met Abid Ali! Really. Remember the cricketer who invades my dreams from a long time ago? Turns out he lives in California. Srini recognized him right away – well, not right away – but at the checkout counter. We had gone to buy some medicines at Walgreens. He had come to fill his prescription. The pharmacist called out, 'Mr Abid Ali,' and Srini whipped around. The man thought Srini was Ali! With this *pattai vibhuti*[11] and all! It was quite funny. When an old gentleman dressed in track pants and a T-shirt came forward and picked up the medication, Srini gave a whoop of delight. He gushed and introduced himself as a big fan and introduced me as a big fan too. I nodded.

The man in front of us was a shadow of the dapper young batsman whose photo Srini had showed me. Shadows are, by and large, not slower than the original. It was a version of the man that was slower, shorter and weaker than the man we knew.

He shook Srini's hand, gave me a namaste and chatted away with Srini. I saw Srini's ears turn pink as he gave his I-don't-find-it-funny-but-I-need-to-impress-you laugh.

He took a picture on his mobile with him, of course, and I was tagged 'PC' on Facebook. What would happen if P.C. Sreeram took a photo? Would it say PC: PC?

Abid Ali has called Srini home one day. I mean, Srini literally invited himself. Now he's going to be 2 feet above the ground for a long, long time. In turn, Srini has invited him to the wedding without discussing it with either Pari or Radha. He's going to get an earful from Pari, I think. Rather, I hope. We've been asked, explicitly, to not randomly invite people.

---

11.   Holy ash. For Lord Shiva and some yogis, the source is cremation grounds. For mortals, it's cow dung.

'This is not like India, where you walk around with a bunch of invitations in your *manja pai*,' were Pari's exact words.

I asked Srini to write down what happened and give it to me on a piece of paper. Srini is what you call a guest blogger, I suppose. I've stuck it here. Abid Ali! Of all the cricketers in the world – him! Maybe it's some sort of sign. I wish I could interpret it though.

Srini's conversation with Abid Ali

I met Sri Syed Abid Ali today at Walgreens, the supermarket. Myself and my wife Smt. Pankajam had walked to Walgreens in order to buy a bottle of cough medication, as Sow. Parineeta had suggested.

After we purchased the required medication we were browsing through the other aisles when I heard a name being called. 'Mr Abid Ali!' My mind immediately went to the young, all-rounder from Hyderabad – the man who danced to calypso music, was the life of the team, and who was born twenty years too early. We celebrate Mr Virat Kohli for his fitness today, but Sri Abid Ali had perfected the art ages ago. He was destined to remain subservient to the spin quartet during the course of his career, which was, unfortunately, cut short after wonderful performances with the bat and ball.

Anyway, as I approached the counter, expecting to encounter Sri Ali, the pharmacist extended the little white bottles to me and I politely declined. A hand came from behind me and took the bottles from the pharmacist, producing the required identification.

I turned to look at Sri Ali, my heart beating fast. I hoped to not have an attack or something and embarrass myself. Thankfully the aforementioned did not happen, and I introduced myself casually. It was him, of course. I knew the minute he opened his mouth to reveal a mouth full of teeth.

We spoke about cricket, the newer generation of players and T-20. I had expected Sri Ali to be against the shorter format, but he was all for it. I suppose one never knows. We promised to stay in touch. As if we were old friends. Sri Ali coaches here, at the Stanford Academy. I would love to send my grandson, Neel. I think he is destined for iPad games only though. Maybe if there is a world cup for that, he will compete.

By our joint request, Smt. Pankajam took a photo of the two of us. I think I sent it to Sekar, my brother, who is a die-hard spin fan.

God willing, we will meet again. Insha Allah!

PS: This really happened. It's not a prank. Ignore the date.

Saturday, 3 April 2015

There's a lot of activity. The wedding's in less than three weeks.

It seems, finally, that Prathik might come here for the wedding. It looks like he might also get a job here or something, I think. Not sure if he'll take it up, because of Sekar's condition. He is doing much better, but I hear it's always around the corner, waiting to pounce on you.

Viswa told us all of this. She always tells us news of this person and that, but sometimes I feel she doesn't tell us about herself. I have no idea what she is up to.

Prathik and Viswa have a special bond. If you only saw them, you'll know immediately what I mean. What they share is eerily like Srini and Pari, only a bit weirder, because they seem to be a couple to the outside world. I hope Prathik has a friend that he can introduce to Viswa. All efforts along those lines have come to a standstill. Sometimes, I'm angry at Pari for taking the focus off Viswa and making a grand spectacle of her own life.

As it is, I am not too thrilled with the priests and everything. What is the need? We met them recently; they have decided on having every ritual we had – even the *nalangu*, the games. You know, the games where a ring is dropped into a pot of milk and both the bride and the groom try to fish it out, and they break *appalam*s over each other's heads, with silk-sari–clad *mami*s begging the clear winner to cut the other some slack and let them win at least one game. Especially if the winning streak is the bride's.

At my wedding I won all those games, even the strength ones, and I was asked, loudly, to go easy on Srini as he was getting flustered. He hated the photos of the *nalangu* and then one day, they mysteriously disappeared. In Pari and Radha's case, I think Radha will win all of them, hands down. If they really compete, that is.

Sunday, 4 April 2015

I'm writing on Sunday itself, because I forget half the things that happen on Sunday by Monday. And Sunday is when everything happens. And Saturday. Actually, more stuff happens on Saturday. Maybe I should write on both days, then.

We're buying clothes for the wedding. I don't know what to say – the girls have bought me an amazing peacock-blue sari, with zari work throughout the body in zigzag patterns. The best part of it is the blouse – it seems to have on it more stones than ration rice! And in different colours! I think I'll need to exercise to simply wear it. Srini's attire takes the cake, though: he has a maroon kurta with a turban. He has been looking at YouTube videos on how to wear them.

After a long debate, Pari decided to also wear a sari. She wanted to do a kurta pyjama, but Radha and a few friends were called in for an 'intervention', as I served them all over-sweet, over-diluted cups of tea. They debated and discussed the nuances of an all-woman wedding.

'You wearing a kurta will send the wrong message,' one of the friends told her.

Most of them, I think, were like Pari and Radha. One of them seemed to be making eyes at Radha.

I wanted to slap that girl hard. The thought threw me off completely. I couldn't hear what they were discussing as my eyes followed hers, anger simmering inside me, threatening to spill over every time she looked at Radha.

I turned to see Srini absorbing every word they were saying. An irritating grin was slapped across his face. Before I could react, one of the girls (not the slap-worthy one) turned to him. 'Uncle, we are people. You don't have to take notes.' I almost whooped in joy as Pari rolled her eyes, gave an 'ah-these-parents' expression and did not meet her father's beseeching eyes.

When I look back at this, this mindfully planned wedding, I wonder. We largely followed the comfortable familiarity of furrowed paths, like the *vagudus*[12] on Pari's and Viswa's heads that automatically showed themselves even after a particularly

12. Centre parting for pigtails.

vigorous oil bath. The path of life really is set. All we have to do is live it. We have a few choices we can make, but by and large, we must earn, save, marry off kids, retire, play with grandchildren, wait for death and when the Buffalo Man comes, embrace him with a smile.

Now, everything is questioned, and perhaps for good reason. Why should I not cut my hair on Tuesdays, one asks. Why should I not enter the kitchen during my period, another asks. I know not, because I wanted no knots. Perhaps it was the mistake that our generation made. So we're making up things that these children strike down with force. Like diligent quality assurance people, they examine every single act of their parents (us) and find in it a flaw or two. They question it and when we come up short, they toss it in the bin. Clearly, these girls have asked of themselves the most basic question of all.

They want to know things: of the world, and of themselves. I might have done okay with the first, but I think I am horrible at the second. Left with no idea of who I am, and in the face of a memory that is crumbling like a Cello bucket left in the hot sun, I will soon be adrift in the deep sea.

Questions are the gateway to discovering yourself. If they were me, these girls would have asked themselves: Why was I unhappy when I went to Sekar's girl-seeing? When the alliance was settled, why did I cry? Why am I thinking of it now?

117

Then, however, I didn't go probing. Like my less-than-sparkling house, it didn't make sense to shine light in corners full of cobwebs.

Tuesday, 21 April 2015

Tomorrow's the wedding. I've shut myself in the bathroom to write. I feel I must record this as it happens, only I don't know how to hold it in my heart forever. New memories are like spirit on my hand. They chill me, make me pay attention, but as soon as I do, they vanish into thin air mixing with the great ether. What might remain is the coolness, or to be more accurate, the memory of coolness against my skin.

The kids are excited. I am finally excited. Prathik has landed. Viswa is here. Srini is right outside. The *sammandhi*s are here, in a hotel, though.

Love is in the air. My Bella Bhakti Group has changed its name to '*Dum dum dum.*' Actually, I changed it, but no one has objected. Or responded.

Amid all this I want to banish the thought of Siva from my mind. I want to not feel for him as a mother-in-law. I want to divorce him ruthlessly, and I want my brain to move forward in time and not only during these rare moments of lucidity.

Wednesday, 22 April 2015

The wedding was magical.

I want to capture this moment. I want to really capture it in my head, you see, not just on my cell phone. I want it to make its way through the pores, capillaries, synapses, veins, arteries, rods, cones, whatever will help me remember. Because I feel this is the last significant thing I will actually record. As if, somehow, things will change irrevocably after tomorrow.

When Pari emerged in her soft pink lehenga and Radha in her deep purple one, both elegant yet completely different, eyes only for each other, Siva on the side, his (I suspect) girlfriend on his arm, Viswa laughing with Radha's brother and a bunch of good-looking chaps, it seemed like the 'Subham' slide at the end of a movie, where the lights are switched on and people get up to go home, after a series of misunderstandings or travesties are righted.

This, the wedding, is the Mount Everest of relationships. Today was about the peak being scaled. There were people who came up to Srini and me and congratulated us, and young girls who came up to us, tears in their eyes, and applauded us, as if we had anything to do with anything. I accepted the praise with grace and not a small amount of guilt.

Oh, and the first dance! It was such a beautiful surprise. When they said 'reception' I imagined it would be something along the lines of an Indian one: the bride and groom arriving late and trying to smile through three hours, while also trying to remember the hundreds of relatives, who, on their part, had overcome horrible traffic and line-cutters to take a meaningless photo and video with the bride and groom. Later, they would go to the dining hall for the ultimate task: standing behind the person having dinner so that they could reserve their spot and hurry along the (current) diner. As you might have guessed, I far prefer the nebulous and illegible wedding ceremony, whose significance was, at the very least, scripted.

Anyway, when Radha told me what the American first dance was all about, my first reaction was to laugh. Srini had come close to blows with a woman who had dared to ask him for a dance at one of his office parties. That created a huge hullabaloo and embarrassment (for Srini, of course), and he had to publicly apologize to the woman for raising his hand. He had never ever danced, and I had danced by myself when I heard about being pregnant with Viswa (Pari was too soon and a shock). I had told her this and we all had a good laugh – all except Pari, that is. The first dance was announced, and I braced myself for the vision of portly Mr Verma dancing with Radha to a slow English number.

So imagine my surprise when the strains of a familiar song blared through the speakers, played by the live band. As I recognized it, I instinctively looked up to see if 'Superstar Rajinikanth' was lit up in serial lights in the background (it was not). Before I could locate Srini, I saw the two of them burst to the centre of the stage – Pari and Srini! Replete with Rajini glasses and lungis, of course! When did they find the time to change? And what was going on?

The audio came on: '*Moochon ko thoda round ghumake...*', and the applause was rowdy.

Srini was dancing the steps, clearly taught by Pari, who was the only person Srini seemed to care about now. His smile behind his dark glasses was reserved for his daughter. He was willing to fight every single instinct of his to see his smile reflected in her. Here was a sun who lived for the moon. Viswa dragged me to the dance floor also. Like Cinderella, I lost one slipper. But I didn't care, for I danced, letting myself go completely. It was as if the movement was thawing me. I felt lighter, as if the atoms in my brain were rapidly rearranging themselves, like one of those ten-rupee kaleidoscopes that Srini got Pari at the trade fair. And then the music slowed down. It segued into a slow number. Now, finally, Radha and her father, I thought. This was going to be a tough act to follow.

121

When the lights came on, there they were – Srini and
Pari – again! To the tune of an English song. I've written
the name somewhere: 'Time of Your Life' by some Green
Day. It was beautiful. Tears are falling on this page. I've
become silly.

When the song ended, Pari was crying. Radha was crying.
Srini was to hand her over to Radha, but just couldn't let go.
His eyes were wet and his shoulders were shaking.

I can't stop bawling now. This is why I said – the picture-
perfect *Subham* was where it should have ended.

I'm just about to sleep, but I can't. It might be all the
adrenaline. Srini said something weird just now though. I
hope he's lying. He said I was surprised to see him. He said
I thought he was Sekar. The circles under his eyes seemed
baggier as he removed his glasses, then turned his back to me
and said, 'You smiled in a way I haven't seen for years.'

He was lying.

Palm Bella Vista, Chennai

Friday, 22 May 2015

I am simply staring at this page. I'm writing words that may mean nothing. I had forgotten about this diary, and Viswa reminded me gently, as if the softness of her words would couch the hard, prickly truth that I had begun to slowly decay. 'Maybe you should try writing in this again, Ma,' she said, picking up her bag to go to Bangalore. 'We'll figure out a way, Ma.' Way where, way for what? As far as I am concerned, there is only one way. Up.

I feel like a goldfish in a glass bowl – people constantly looking in, and every contour of mine magnified. I just want to be left alone most days. Just to live quietly and not attract any attention to the fact that I am still here.

Look at what happened when Pari wanted to shout from the rooftops that she was there and living life on her terms. Srini couldn't take it, is what.

I will not speak with her, Pari. And I wish Viswa didn't call me twice every day. There is really nothing that she can say that will change it all.

Once, ages ago, I saw a cow tethered to a post and thought it was so inhuman. My father told me that the cow never walks out that far, and it never really knows that it is tied, so, in a sense, is it really tethered? Now I know that Srini was my tether. I've walked too far away (or rather, he has). I can feel the strain. And God knows I am surprised that I was, in fact, tethered, without ever knowing it.

Monday, 25 May 2015

It's all the same. Viswa calls me now and then, and I've asked her again not to call me so often. The Bella Bhakti Group ladies won't let me be, and I go there purely out of habit. Kamala goes on as if everything is the same. They talk about everything but Pari, as if everything is not connected intricately. They ask about the kids, but studiously avoid mention of Pari and Radha. And Srini, as if I will simply break down if they do. Maybe I will.

Monday, 1 June 2015

I don't know what to say now. Everyone's gone and it's just me here. I've just been cleaning the house, preparing myself to go to the Vishnupuram Retirement Community.

I think I'm going to miss this house.

The house is so lonely now.

I have been forgetting so much since Srini. It's time to visit the doctor and maybe up my medication. I have to call Viswa. I sometimes wonder what Pari is up to. I can't call her, obviously. It has been months since I spoke with her. Since Srini, actually.

Friday, 5 June 2015

I received another call from the ladies. For this year's summer party by the pool. They told me that it will be good for me to get out. I don't think so. I will simply stay at home. In any case, I have to leave shortly.

Monday, 15 June 2015

I think that maybe I must re-start this diary. Maybe things will become better. Now, though, I'm left with nothing but my memory, which insists on traveling back in time – back several decades, in fact.

Right now, all I want to do is lie down by the *aala maram* Pillayar at Nandhimangalam. The breeze beneath the tree – nothing can beat that. Just whiling away time, talking about this and that, the way we did when we were kids. Blazing summer days with the Kollidam flowing by. Even today, I miss Kollidam and Her constant presence that went unnoticed unless you left Nandhimangalam. We went to school walking on Her banks, cried our tears into Her waters, we bathed, played, fought and made up next to Her. We depended on Her for our sustenance, and She, in turn, fed us and clothed us and also, like a real-life mother, somewhere, hated us just a little bit, for being so dependent on Her. Just as a reminder of Her power, She would take someone away every year. At least one. We weren't supposed to mess with Her when She was in *roudram*:[13] PMS, if you will – as She charged Her way through the path. She tried to break the banks that defined Her, and sometimes, She even succeeded. If any one of us dared to go beyond, dared to disturb Her, She would show

13.   Anger, not very *shobha*-giving for a woman, except Gods.

no mercy. Every person in our village of Nandhimangalam was related to someone who was taken by Her. It was as if she had a pact with Dhanvantri to take out those outside the bell curve. While He took away the weaker ones – the malnourished, the deformed – the ones She took were almost always the strongest, the valorous and the bravest.

Ammini was my first friend She took away.

We were sitting, one November afternoon, in the shade of the banyan tree under which stood a Pillayar shrine. It was after school and Ammini had brought me there, saying she had an important secret to tell me. To seven-year-olds, it generally meant something embarrassing about a friend, like bed-wetting, or some five-year-old who still drank milk from their mother. I had tried to pry it out of her on the way, but she would not tell me.

She got up and I followed her on the bund, when she turned around suddenly and looked me up and down. 'You won't believe it!' was all she said, turning right back and walking ahead, her book bag slung on her left shoulder as mine was on the right. Like a dog investigating the suitability of every single place for excretion, Ammini was apparently on the lookout for the perfect spot where she could 'tell Pankajam the secret'.

She examined the *aala maram* and rejected it and its hoary history, and went further down to another one with no apparent history of its own. Maybe she wanted to create

127

some. She walked around the tree, making sure there was no one listening, and faced me. Her eyes were twinkling with excitement, the way they did when she was about to do something dangerous. Then she sat down solemnly, the way she had seen the old priest at the Ayyanar temple do, and a giggle bubbled up from within me.

(I can't believe I remember this so clearly.)

I sat in front of her, clearing the space between us of little stones and pebbles.

'Pankajam,' she began. 'You must not tell anyone about this, okay?'

I was sick of all the preamble. I told her as much.

'*Illa, di*. It's very important. I feel unsafe even telling you this.' She looked around, as if to emphasize her fear. Not for nothing was she always selected to play the lead in the class drama.

'I don't know how to start,' she said, making little knots at the edge of her *pavadai*,[14] the tuck having been opened several times over, revealing its past in bands of progressively darker shades of blue. I remembered the *pavadai* from three years ago.

14. Traditionally a long skirt, usually worn until puberty, after which the transitional *pavadai–dhavani* (breasts covered, little bit of hip show) until the wedding, and then the sari. Now making a comeback as a style statement for adults, sans breast cloth, because, well, that's just too many layers.

'Come on already,' I said, irritably. 'It's going to be something stupid only.'

'No, no, not at all.'

I turned and made as if to get up.

She reached up and pulled at my shoulders, and I sat back down.

She leaned forward conspiratorially. 'Do you know how babies happen?'

I was supremely uninterested in the topic, of course. I'd assumed they just grew inside you and shot out, like seedlings and plants.

'I don't know,' I said and shrugged.

'You've seen a boy, no? Your brother?'

I said nothing.

'You know how they have a *kunju*? It's not only for pissing, you know.'

I didn't know where this was leading. Surely nowhere good. She cleared her throat.

'It seems they make babies by putting it into girls, *di*,' she whispered.

'What?' I shouted, and she hushed me.

'Yes, yes,' she said urgently, finally having got my attention. 'All of us.'

'But putting it inside girls means...where?'

It was her turn to shrug. 'Guess. One hole.'

It could be somewhere down there, I knew, but I had no clue. But when Paati died, Amma had told me that there were nine holes in the body through which life could pass. There were the nostrils, ears and eye sockets (each two numbers), the mouth and the rectum. I don't know where the ninth was. Perhaps where I peed? I didn't like to think of anyone's life passing through there; so I hadn't thought much about it. What was this new thing she was saying?

I think I ran over the first three holes out loud, and Ammini just shut her ears laughing. A second later, she turned serious. 'One uncle told me, *di*. He said I should not tell anyone. If I did, bad things will happen to me. So maybe I should not tell you now.' Her face contorted and the mirth of a few seconds ago drained away visibly, like an over-squeezed *sathukudi*.

She made to get up and I got up too. 'Tell me, no. Nothing will happen.'

'That uncle showed me, *di*. He said he could do all kinds of black magic. Now I am scared.'

'Don't be. All right, don't tell me ever. Happy?'

Her face darkened more. 'You also don't tell anyone, okay? Don't want any bad luck for you also, no?'

I laughed then. 'You are just over-imagining these things. Nothing will happen. Come, let's go home.'

'*Nee po*, *di*. I'll come in a few minutes.'

'I'll also go in a few minutes.'

'You go. I will just wade in the water and come.'

'It's not safe.'

'You are such a scared girl.'

'And you are stupid, wanting to go like that.'

'Scared. Scared. Scared. Look at me. I am going to go into the water.'

'Stop it. I am not scared.'

'Scared. Scared. Scared. Go away and hide.'

'You are mean and evil.'

'Amma told me Kollidam is like my mother. So you stay here on Her bank, all scared, while I go and meet Her.'

'Fine. I don't want to be arguing with you.'

'Great, so go home. Why are you standing here?'

'Ammini, come up. The water is running fast.'

'So you also run fast. Run home fast.'

I did exactly as she said, vowing never to speak to her again. And that's exactly what happened.

I waited for her to come back to me. Only she never came. Instead news came when we were having dinner that there was a search party out for her, near the river.

I rushed, wiping my hands on my *pavadai*. I ran past the milling crowds. I wanted them all out of there. But my friend was nowhere to be seen. I went to the riverbank, retracing our path of the afternoon, and later waited by the bund, talking to the police. I was the last one to have seen her alive.

Last. Alive. They sounded like the end, but I had a tiny sliver of hope that I focused on, however thin. Soon life without Ammini began, as if that moment was but an ad break.

I could not let go, obviously. It seemed like she was on a forever trip to her mama's house; wherever I went, I looked for her.

For years, crowds were groups of randomly moving organisms, like in those Harpic ads, as I looked to identify only one person in them. It became a habit, and it seemed one eye of mine was always scanning people. In my spare time I'd imagine how our meeting would happen. I'd run into her, toppling her bags, and she would look up unexpectedly. I'd obviously say, 'Sorry,' only to meet her glorious eyes smile back at me. Or I'd be on my way to New Delhi, and she would be on the train, begging, and when she looked at me, palms outstretched, I'd grasp them and press them together, hugging her tight. In all of these scenarios, her face remained the same: that of a narrow-eyed, seven-year-old girl with pigtails. Why did I get angry that day? Why didn't I just stay?

I can still smell the Margo soap on her. My mother would not buy soap (only *kadalai maavu*) and Ammini sometimes got some stock from her mama. I remember us oddly rubbing our hands and legs against each other, so I would get the Margo smell on my body too. Margo soap on Ammini. The one smell I can never forget. Even if all my memory leaves me. I wonder if Margo soap is still available in the market.

132

Vishnupuram Retirement Community, Chennai

Monday, 22 June 2015

I hate this place. I want our apartment back.

I hate the fact that I seem to be going in circles all the time.

I can see that I look familiar to some of the people here. Their facial muscles relax when they see me and they are not curious the way they were when they first saw me. I hate that memory seems not to be digital – that I can't, like a VHS tape, run a cleaning liquid and retrieve that hazy image that I just cannot recall. I hate that even as you peel off the layers of someone and are getting to their core, finding out what really makes them tick, trying to anchor them in space, time, or visually, they are gone. I hate that I'm not sure what 'gone' even means. I hate that all the girls here call me 'paati' whether they're fifteen or twenty or thirty-five. I hate that a face comes to me unbidden and I look for it around me, like in a video game, and I hate not finding it and not knowing whether it is because the person is only in my head or just simply dead. I hate that I'm one of the youngest here so I am usually talking with someone as old as my father would be, if he were alive. I love that he died like Srini, in his sleep, his life just snipped, cut clean, so his body and mind left in sync. I love how similar one day is to the next, though. It's hard earth, sure, but constant furrowing will hopefully create those creases like the one on my forehead.

The sameness, mostly, helps me remember things, things like writing this diary.

The only other diary I remember reading was one serialized novel in *Kalki* – how Sekar and I used to discuss it and tear it apart. I think I'll stop for the day. I remember enough.

Monday, 29 June 2015

I think I've become worse in some things but better at others. I want to go back home, which is all locked up. But then, I was the one who insisted on this. Maybe I'll go back and ask Viswa to take me in. But how will she manage? She needs to get a house-husband. Maybe I can look for one of those. I'll check with Malathi here at the centre and see if she can get me time on the computer. You won't believe the waiting list for that thing. Apparently, premium members have laptops in their rooms (with free Wi-Fi, of course). How much Srini would have enjoyed that!

Srini, swiping and swiping. I still have his phone. His last messages, mostly WhatsApp forwards, memes with Vadivelu and Parthiban. It's run out of charge I considered putting my SIM in it and using it, but like that girl in that SPB movie – you know, who has her dead mother's breath in an air pillow and attacks her father's fiancée for deflating it? – I want to preserve some part of him as him. That's why they bury people, I think. So there is some place we can go to, something we can touch and see, something physical to remember the person. A tombstone is exactly that. A physical anchor of the memory of a person. When you burn someone, you only have memories. And that's a slippery thing. I remember all sorts of things from some distant past, as if it were yesterday. Why, I can nearly taste and smell the brinjals from home, their dark purple lending them a certain gravitas that the bright *ujala* brinjals lack. The others, the green ones, were too like green vegetables to be taken seriously, and the fat brinjals were imports; I only used them, years later, for *baingan bharta*, which was the only brinjal dish that the *bharta*[15] would eat.

15. Husband.

Sekar liked it too, I think. Nowadays I seem to confuse the two – Srini and Sekar. It's all one big mess in my head, like that ball of wool I used in my one and only attempt at knitting. It was when I was pregnant with Viswa and I needed to feel it. Feel pregnant. I saw an old women's magazine (the magazine was old) which featured an elegant woman, the pregnancy dome clearly visible, happily knitting something for her unborn child. She seemed so at peace, and she was smiling also, so I thought I must try it. It was surely likely that knitting gave the woman the sort of peace that I craved, to calm my nerves and hormones and whatnot?

So long story short, I could never become that image. If anyone had taken a picture of me, it would have been the perfect opposite of that one – hair dishevelled, wool all messy, face irritated, and the knitting needles poking the belly from all angles (hopefully not damaging the baby).

But what was it that I began with? Sekar and Srini. I am simply mixing the two up. I find I'm missing Sekar and then it hits me that I can't miss him – Srini's the one who is gone.

I want to remember most days, and what happened. But the one night I want to forget, I can't seem to. I can't forget that the day after the wedding, I woke up next to Srini, brushed my teeth, and tiptoed out of the bedroom, thinking that I would like some coffee by myself before everyone else woke up. That in half an hour, people had started calling him 'body' as if Srini had just exited himself and left.

That his last words to me were, 'You smiled in a way I haven't seen for years.' And that the last thing I had called him was Sekar.

Wednesday, 8 July 2015

Today was a good day. What I remember of it, at least. It would be boring if all I said was that I went to Sekar's house, so I'm writing down details – filling in stuff where there's a blank. What is memory but some brain connections? What is creativity but the same?

It had been a while since I went out of the retirement home. I'll just call it what it is: an old-age home! To tell the truth, the average age sort of beats you down. I wanted to get outside to smell the real smell of air, not the putrid smell of sweat and bodily fluids mixed with talcum powder and phenyl. So I figured I would go meet Sekar. It had been a long time since we talked. His treatment is going well, they said.

I asked Vasantha to book me one of those cabs. They have one Indica taxi guy who is used to taking the old people around. So he doesn't mind the chatter, I suppose. I don't like to chat too much though. I used to like it but not any more. I usually close my eyes when I'm in a cab. It's easier. When I got off the cab, I saw Renuka waiting for me by the door. It's not like I'm a child, and this irritates me; the way seemingly normal people always try to take care of me, as if their worrying is going to help me any.

Renuka walked to the gate and welcomed me, looking perfect as always in a starched sari. I knew Sekar still had a few more sessions of chemo to go. So how did she find the time and energy to starch her saris? It must just be in her DNA. I half-expected Sekar to call out in his booming voice, 'What have you got for me?' Sometimes he would even use 'Pankajam *manni*', instead of just '*manni*', earning a glare from Srini and a smile from me.

There was, of course, no voice. I walked in, quickly handing over the packet of sweets from A2B.

'He's not supposed to eat sweets,' Renuka said, and went to the kitchen where, I knew, she would arrange the sweets in a plate for me.

'It's for you, Renuka,' I called after her.

I made my way to the bedroom, where Sekar likely was. As I neared the door of the room, I heard him, *'Vaango, manni.'*

There he was, thinner than I remembered him. But smiling.

138

I had never been alone with him in a room, had I? I don't remember.

'How are you?' I asked and hesitated as I took the foldable steel chair that was placed next to the bed, it seemed, for this very purpose.

'Fine, fine, they tell me I'll be up and running in no time.' He added, 'What have you got for me?'

I winced. 'Sweets, Sekar. Sorry. I know you can't eat them.'

He laughed. 'Why sorry? There are other people in this house too.'

We sat there in silence for a bit. I looked at him and wondered what it was that seemed different now. His eyes were closed and I wondered if he had fallen asleep, until I saw a teardrop escape his shut eyelids. I felt Renuka behind me and turned to see two plates in her hand. One of them featured the *kaju katli* from A2B neatly arranged in a geometric pattern, and the other Milk Bikis arranged in a fan.

Sekar opened his eyes too. 'Take it, take it,' he egged me on as I gingerly took a piece of the sweet and one biscuit, spoiling the biscuit fan in the process. Renuka walked away, calling out, 'I have to go to the shop, you keep talking.'

'Where does she find the time?' I whispered, pointing to the now-broken fan pattern.

'I don't know,' he whispered back. 'There isn't much to do around here, I suppose.'

'So...' I said, looking around the lightly furnished house. Photos of my parents-in-law and their parents evaluated us from their perches in every room.

I remembered how it was when Renuka first came into the house. This house. The house that Sekar has purchased from Srini, after Prathik was born. The house that held so much of me within its walls that I was surprised I could let go. The house where, really, I grew up. And it was still teaching me lessons. Only, I wasn't sure I would remember them.

In the corner, where Sekar's bureau now stood, used to be a desk – the desk where I sometimes wrote some poetry to occupy myself. There, in the kitchen, I learned how to cook. In the bedroom, where Sekar now lay, I learned so much and unlearned even more.

Sekar, that boy who argued point after point following me around with a plate in his hand, who navigated politics and literature with ease, who mirrored me in many ways, was now ill. His voice could not even rise above the hum of the fridge. My hands automatically went to his head, as I patted his head thrice. All I could think was that my hands felt strange there. He looked at me too, pain clear in his eyes. I withdrew my hand quickly.

'*Manni*,' he said slowly. 'What do you think is the point of life?'

'Mostly that we don't have to talk about things like this.' I tried to keep a straight face.

'But really, tell me.'

I was not used to talking like this with Sekar, not when it mattered at least. There were always philosophical discussions we had, buoyed by youth, encouraged by the seemingly infinite time we had. But that was all just the 'trials' of gully cricket. When the bowler yelled, 'All reals – first ball,' you better keep your head down and bat responsibly. This was the 'all reals'.

'I don't know, Sekar.' He had always told me it was unfair – that I was allowed to use his name by itself, while he couldn't. 'I've been accused of only caring about myself, and sometimes I think I probably do. Does one have to worry about others? Can one just not live for oneself and die?'

'You remember how you used to talk about your friends over at Bella?' He breathed deeply.

'I might have said a lot of things. I was, I am, a rude old woman.'

'No, no. It was something to do with their TVs. You said they had the latest HD TVs, but all they watched on it was mega serials.'

That did sound like me. 'So?'

'It's like that, I sometimes feel. We're not using our capability. We're given this human form with all its related senses, like that high-end TV. And we only eat, watch TV and sleep like any other animal? That doesn't seem right.'

141

'What are you saying, Sekar? What do you think life is all about then?'

'I don't know, *manni*. I feel maybe, just maybe, there is a purpose to it all, you know. Service, maybe?' It was a question, and it was obvious he had had a lot of time to think about it, but he had no answer.

'Or maybe we are meant to just live on this planet and leave it as we found it.'

He laughed. 'That's certainly what you would say! It's the easier solution.'

'What do you mean? You think my life has been easy?'

'No, *manni*. It has not. But when faced with problems, you've always done that.'

'What are you talking about?'

'Make a joke. Hide. Run away. Isn't that what you do?'

My heart was beating wildly. I knew he was trying to get at something and that something was peeking out from the hidden corners of my memory. I closed my eyes, trying to remember, or forget, both of which seemed impossible now.

I heard a noise at the gate and stood up abruptly.

'Sekar, I need to go.'

'Run away,' he whispered, even as I grabbed my handbag and ran to the hall, where Renuka (and sanity) were waiting for me.

'*Manni*, what's the matter?' she asked, even as I gestured wildly and ran outside. Thank God she did not have to give me *vethala paaku*.[16]

Once outside, I took deep breaths. I turned the corner past a waiting auto driver and a fruit seller. I leaned against the bus stop pillar and got into the waiting taxi.

I looked outside the window at the dusty roads that led to Sekar's house. At the flies buzzing about the sweetshop counter, unbothered by the black cloth that was used to shoo them away. Like we were shooed away before Krishna Jayanti. To steal a sweet before Amma or Paati got to know about it was a feat in itself. Mani, Ammini's brother, was the one who came home every year and tried that. He would wait for the opportune moment and swoop in on the closed dabbas, somehow timing the opening of the dabba with another, sharper sound to distract Paati, who had very sharp ears. In a split second, a few *seedai*s would be out of the dabba and in his hands.

Of course, Vasu, my brother, the copycat, would try the same thing and every year, he would get caught. Nearly beaten too. It was the year after Ammini that Paati and Amma started counting the *seedai*s and *murukku*s they made. Mani never came after that and the *seedai*s remained intact, just like that.

16. Women other than widows traditionally receive vermillion and betel leaf and nut when they leave a house.

Monday, 13 July 2015

Viswa's here. She said she plans to be here for a while. She doesn't talk much and I don't ask her much. I get the feeling something's the matter with her. Or me. Or both. I am not sure what. The first doctor's visit has happened today. I understand there are many more.

They've also asked me to leave the room more often, so I'm writing this from the 'activity room'. All the activity you'll see here is the slow movement of hands and legs, and coming here always makes me think I've entered another world.

Do you remember how you could play the audio on the Walkmans (or is it walkmen) slower? We used to be able to do that with those VHS tapes also. Srini used to pause all the fight sequences and play them frame by frame to show me how the heroes did not actually hit the villains. I got the idea after the first couple of those, but didn't tell him. I let him think I didn't realize. I suppose I liked the warm cosiness of his presence and the familiarity of routine.

I feel a bit self-conscious in the activity room. The room is bright, sunlight streaming in from the large French windows. The room is air-conditioned, and the spot of light on the sofa strikes me like a warm cup of tea on my tongue. To my right, there's a table with a couple of chairs. It's all dusted and new. On the table is an incomplete Eiffel Tower puzzle, at least 1,000 pieces. The rest of the pieces are in a box, and there's a photo of a woman on the chair in front of it. There's a small bunch of marigolds hanging from the top of the frame down to her eyes, just about masking them. I want to reach out and part the flowers, look at her face, if only to see if I recognize her. My hands are also itching to take the box with the remaining pieces and finish the puzzle. I wonder what the acceptable period of mourning and memoriam might be. It can't be too long; this place is full of exits.

Viswa has gone out somewhere. These days I'm not so worried about her marriage. Maybe that's what self-preservation is. Viswa has told the nurse and helpers what I'm supposed to do, and they ask me every day about my activities. They are also monitoring me, I'm sure, from the corners of the curtains and the spaces of the staircase.

There's a couple of other things too that I can do – the Sudoku and the Six Differences thing. Plus the puzzles. I wish I had the patience for these huge puzzles. I think there's some sort of evaluation that's going to happen at some point. If there was a way to cheat, I would. Increasing the medication only makes me sleep more and more. I want to stay alive. I mean awake.

Tuesday, 14 July 2015

There's no other way to say it, so I'll just say it: Ammini is here! At least I think it was her. I was minding my own business, lost in my useless thoughts in the garden, when I saw her enter a waiting car. I suppose she came with someone, but I have no idea who.

I went and asked the office, but they said they cannot tell me anything and that all information was confidential. I will get a look in somehow. They must have registered her address or something. If she knew I was here, surely she'd choose this place? Maybe I can convince the people here with that logic.

In the evening, the family came over for some sort of celebration. I don't know what it was for. Viswa was here and so were Sekar and Renuka. And there was a young boy with them, clean-shaven head and all. The boy was not with Viswa I think, because he knew every single detail of Sekar's treatment. So maybe he was Sekar's nurse or something. Anyway, the good news is that Sekar's much better and they haven't found anything in the latest tests they took.

Renuka, of course, brought me the same thing she has brought me whenever she visited us since she was married:

a kilo of the fruit of the season. Nowadays, though, since apples are in season all year round, it's usually apples. One kilo apples, in a green plastic bag. 'Why, ma, all this formality?' I said for the thousandth time and she replied for the same-th time, 'This is no formality. We want to give you this.'

Sekar smirked on the side. 'You know what, Renuka, you should get her the latest *Mills and Boons* book.'

Actually, he was right. Books would be nice. The library here is very limited. And old, like the people here.

Viswa kept stealing glances at me. I wonder why. It was as if she was asking me to judge something. Was it that boy? I simply could not see that boy as her boyfriend.

At the end of it all, though, I was exhausted. I wanted to push all of them out and sleep. I very nearly did. I encouraged them to book a taxi even though it was quite expensive.

I didn't have dinner. I'm writing this instead. Viswa has gone to the guest house, I hope alone. Actually, it doesn't really matter any more. But Ammini! I know I'm too tired, but can I sleep? I doubt it.

Tuesday, 21 July 2015

I might be writing everyday but there is not much to report. All I seem to be able to do properly is record food. This tasteless, bland, low-salt, low-sugar food is tiring. What I wouldn't give for my mother's *vathakuzhambu* now. Gleaming like the water on the roads after a heavy rain, the colours of the rainbow reflected on a base red film of gingelly oil, a shadow of the taste explosion to come. Now I'm feeling bad.

Wednesday, 22 July 2015

We had beans, sambar, rasam and the usual salad for lunch. For dinner, we had two tiffin items: khichdi and dosai. It's on the board.

Thursday, 23 July 2015

It turns out I don't recognize the lady who was doing the jigsaw puzzle. We had salad and vegetable rice for lunch. I think we had a sweet too. For dinner, we had *arisi upma*. It had less salt, even lesser than usual.

Friday, 24 July 2015

I have nothing to report.

Saturday, 25 July 2015

There was a feast today for lunch. I think it was the sixteenth-day ceremony for the jigsaw lady. The jigsaw was packed off overnight a few days ago. I would have at least felt good finishing something that woman started. My only chance at finishing the 1,000-piece puzzle has gone.

Tuesday, 28 July 2015

It finally happened. Ammini is a resident here! What are the chances? I really cannot believe it. Our meeting was not as fancy as I'd imagined it all these years. No trains, no girl with pigtails, no teary-eyed reunion. I was at the dining table, having lunch, when one of the caretakers came around introducing her. I didn't even recognize her, nor was I paying attention. People check in and out all the time.

She was fidgeting with the edge of her sari – it was a crisp Bengal cotton sari. She looked worried, and I smiled. I told her this was a nice place; she will like it. Even then, I was talking to her without knowing who she was. It just didn't strike me. Perhaps she was frozen in my head, as a seven-year-old. She looked so different the other day when she had come to inquire after me. But then, who can trust my memory?

She sat down right next to me and I was surprised. I like my aloneness. I don't want anyone coming into my circle, and she didn't even ask whether she could. She only kept staring at me. The caretaker left, considering her job done, palming a new resident off to an old one.

I moved the chair just an inch away from her and attacked my lunch.

'I have eaten already,' she said, in spite of my ignoring her.

Unable to take her looking at me, I had to talk to her. 'Do you know me?' I asked.

'Seems like it. Are you, by any chance, from near Kumbakonam?'

Immediately my heart raced like a horse on the Guindy course. 'Yes.' I was barely breathing. I pushed away the plate of food.

'Pankajam?' I could see her looking closely at me, her eyes narrowed.

I thought my heart would explode. I didn't know what to do – shouting seemed odd, and we were awkwardly seated for a hug. I didn't even know when the cry escaped me. It was a long moan, and I must have terrified the others for when I woke up I was back in my room. Viswa was by my side.

Saturday, 1 August 2015

The second doctor's visit happened. This was, apparently, a behavioural neurologist. I think it means 'behaves like a neurologist, but not a real one'.

Basically, she gave me a bunch of what she called cognitive tests. Some of them were fun. I had to find a particular vegetable in a garden patch. I had to make out shapes on a page. I had to quickly pick the words from a screen. It was all done on the computer and she made the vegetable patch thing more and more difficult. I enjoyed it.

Afterwards she spoke only to Viswa, as if I was some clay. I wish that the feeling of the memory went away with the memory. Most times, though, that doesn't happen. The feeling of the memory remains, like the rocks at the bottom of the river, even as the memory itself is washed away almost immediately.

Sometimes, it's nice that my memory's slowly fading away. I might even ignore the increased dosage. There's a reason I remember some things and not others. Viswa has taken great pains for, well, everything, really, and I might continue this diary for a bit just for her. Otherwise, the doctor (if she is even that) came across as snobbish. What she has suggested though is bound to be fun: more fun than this journal business anyway: video games. Viswa has bought me a tablet of the electronic kind! I did that joke to death (Bring that tablet/ finally a tablet I like/I have to charge this tablet instead of the other way around, etc. I even tried a 'keeping tabs on me' one). I think Viswa wants to move back to Bangalore soon just to escape my jokes.

I cannot wait to tell Ammini all of this. I haven't seen her since that first meeting. I must have been too busy with Viswa. These medicines must be interfering with my state of mind. I asked Viswa, and she did not give a convincing answer. I hope Ammini is still here. She can't be gone; not again. Maybe she is put off by Viswa. She can be abrasive, this girl of mine. After she leaves for Bangalore, I'll go meet Ammini.

Sunday, 2 August 2015

I've never wished so much that someone leave me. It's about time Viswa left to take care of her life. Viswa wants to stay here in Chennai for some time. 'I can work from home. I'll find a job here,' she says. 'There is absolutely no need. Leave me alone,' I want to scream sometimes.

On top of all this, Pari called. I didn't want to talk to her. What is the point, really? All that wedding tension is what pushed Srini off the edge, right? It finally took Srini away.

Viswa insisted I talk to her, but I pushed the phone away. She force-fed me pictures from Neha's birthday party, from her phone. The four of them are a nice happy family. I vaguely wonder who Radha likes more. Do the kids even think of Radha as a mother?

Neha looked pretty, her face polished in the way American kids' faces are. She prepared herself for the cake cutting, taking a deep breath, as if she were to plunge into the pool. Under the pink princess frosting, I could see that it was a chocolate cake.

As Viswa scrolled through the pictures of happy children and adults, the cake feeding and the samosa madness, one picture stuck with me. I'm unable to shake it out of my head, no matter how hard I try. It's as if the trying is making the image stick harder to my brain. In it, Pari, dressed in a white top and jeans, is glaring at me. She is unmindful of the guests and her daughter, even of Radha, who are all in the background and out of focus. She has eyes only for me. She is looking directly at me, the way she did that morning. The morning that…Srini…left. She said nothing all the time I was there, all the time I spent in a daze, wondering what we should do with Srini. We eventually cremated him of course, returning to India with nothing but a jar of ashes. An urn, they called it.

I hurriedly hand the phone back to Viswa. Her eyes, accusing, piercing, sad and knowing. I don't want to talk to her. I don't want to be reminded. With enough time and ignoring, it will automatically heal. No need to go poking into compost piles. They will do what nature intended.

Just let things be. It will all automatically disappear. Like my memories. Keep them buried.

I want to be left alone. Viswa is always with me – when I wake up, during lunch, and even on my walks. I can barely write this diary. It's a wonder she doesn't follow me to the bathroom.

I'll have to tell her, gently, somehow, that she has to go. Ammini is here now.

Monday, 3 August 2015

I am free! Viswa was asked to move to the guest house here. She has been around for a few days now. She decided to move to our Bella apartment instead. It's still furnished, the house. She asked me around a hundred times whether I wanted to go with her. I didn't, of course. Right after she left, after breakfast, I went to the recreation room to see if I could find Ammini. She wasn't there.

I returned at lunch, and still couldn't spot her. I'll try again during the evening. She will come for her walk, I am sure. Maybe she is also stuck in her room.

Viswa keeps calling me and asks me questions of increasing difficulty. As if I don't know that she is testing me.

Tuesday, 4 August 2015

I finally broke and talked to Pari. Viswa came in the morning, and by then there were about five missed calls from Pari. She has always called me regularly, even if I never picked up the phone. Since I returned, I wondered how many calls I had ignored. She messaged me on WhatsApp. I blocked her.

I wonder if Ammini is doing this to teach me a lesson. I've told her about Pari and how I'm not talking to her. She pursed her thin lips but did not say another word. Is she deliberately avoiding me and pushing me to reconcile with Pari? To see Ammini again, I'll need to let go.

'Viswa, call Pari for me. Maybe I should talk to her. She has been calling. Or maybe you can call her and give me the phone.'

Viswa looked at the time. 'Ma, it will be too late for her. Maybe tomorrow.'

'It's only ten there. I am sure she would not have slept yet.'

She walked away, dialling a number. She must have told her sister that their mother was finally ready to talk. When she returned, phone in hand, I reached out for it. I didn't know my fingers trembled. Maybe it's a side effect of these new medicines. I am sure I did not imagine Viswa's hesitation in handing it over to me.

The conversation felt like a journey. Through her questions about my health and Vishnupuram, our comments about Viswa and the disappearing possibility of her matrimony, our shared memories of the man who bound us together even in his absence, we hoped to eventually reach home, even if we were lost without our pole star.

Wednesday, 5 August 2015

I didn't see Ammini at lunch. Like an idiot, I did not ask her for her name. Official name, that is. Surely, she changed her name. If you're looking to start a new life in a new place, you will likely start with changing your name. There is the problem – I basically don't know her name.

She doesn't come down to lunch anymore. An attendant always comes to lunch with me. I suppose Viswa has upgraded me or something. I asked the attendant about Ammini. She asked me for the room number, which I'd forgotten. I described her in detail, but she did not recall anyone like that. She is worse than I am!

Thursday, 6 August 2015

I asked the office here about Ammini. They don't know anyone like that, they said. I was about to ask them for the admission register to see the pictures, because I was certain by now that she had changed her name and told me but this stupid memory of mine does not allow me to remember. Maybe it's written somewhere in this diary. After writing this, I'll read it all again.

By the way, I don't like the girl at the reception. She was so rude to me. 'Will you be like that with your own grandmother?' I asked her.

'I am worse,' she said, then laughed. I could see her mind working: *what can this old lady do? She will forget in a minute and then what? In any case, will people believe her or me?* Little does she know that my memory is not as bad as I let people think. Most of the time, when I don't want to talk about something, I pretend like I don't remember.

I wonder, however. If these people in this old-age home are so rude when I am standing right in front of them, breathing fire, how will they be when I am lying down and no longer breathing? Will they do my *karyam* as planned? Viswa has paid for the costly package, from what I understand. Maybe she wants one parent to get a proper send-off.

I called Sekar and told him what I was worried about. He laughed to my face. My ear, really.

'That's what you are worried about?'

'You know, we have paid for it.'

'Okay, okay. I will remember. But mark my words: you will outlive us all.'

I never spoke about mortality with anyone – least of all Sekar. Suddenly, without warning, I felt a stone in my throat. Since Srini, he had been punctual about calling me and making sure I was okay. He would call every Sunday, as if the days of the week mattered to us. He would make

Renuka and Prathik speak with me too – short conversations, but enough to let me know I had a net below my dangerous circus act. I told him about meeting Ammini.

'Really? Your best friend Ammini? The one who was washed away?'

I ignored the words he used. 'Yes, yes.'

'Wow. What a small world! Seems impossible. Where was she all this while?'

'I didn't ask her. Why ask questions you might not want to know the answers to?'

There was silence. Then slowly a sigh, and then, 'Of course.'

Friday, 7 August 2015

I met her again today. Phew!

I'm walking around with a small notepad – one of those things you get for eleven rupees, and a pencil. Thank God I do that now – I have noted down her name also. Ganga. It's weird – why she would name herself after another water body is beyond me. That too, a north Indian river?

I was sitting in the recreation room, late afternoon or so, trying to read *Ananda Vikatan*. I like to read next to the window, but turns out many people do. So I sat at the table in the centre of the room facing the window. Just as I looked up from some useless news about film stars, I saw her framed by the window. It's times like this that I believe in karma. The exact same time. A second later, or a foot that way or this, and I would have missed her completely.

Of course I ran outside. I stood, panting, and she responded with a smile.

'*Ennanga*, Pankajam?' she asked.

I laughed at her formal address. '*Ennanga'va?*'

'Okay, Panku. How are you?'

'I am fine. Where did you disappear?'

She said nothing. She simply said we would meet every day at the same time: around four.

'Why can't I meet you earlier? Where do you have breakfast, Ammu?'

'Oh, I have it in my room. No one is allowed.'

There was something else about Ammini: she stood straight, and answered in clips. She wasn't the girl whose movements were as free-flowing as her *pavadai*. Something was naturally royal about her, something that made hers the final word in a conversation.

I didn't want to ask her about what happened after she was washed away. It didn't matter, did it? Not for lack of wanting to know. We encircled it several times like it was a funeral pyre, and then just let it be. The past can be left where it belongs.

Saturday, 8 August 2015

I went and found out where Ammini's room was. She had warned me against it, but I could not resist. It is true that I am not allowed in that wing. It is at some higher security level. I wonder why. Maybe she became a princess or something? She said she has no family, but surely someone raised her? None of that matters. The fact is that she cannot meet me as she pleases: only at four o'clock.

At four o'clock, per our plan, I met her. I have set an alarm at 3:30, so I can freshen up before meeting her.

We spoke about life at home in Nandhi, and it was great to go down memory lane. We must have been loud, because other residents were staring at us. I stared right back – no one was going to spoil my time with my friend. A friend whom I had found after such a long search.

'Why didn't you come back?'

'I don't know. I just couldn't. I was already gone.'

I don't quite know what that means, but I understand.

I tell her that her brother was in the army, and that her parents left. She seems uninterested in any of that. And so we go back to talking about life in the village.

We sometimes talk for hours, mostly about old times. I am sure she tells me about her life, but I suppose my eroded memory forgets the details. So I suppose she tells me again.

Sunday, 9 August 2015

I made a big decision today. Ammini and I can move back to Bella Vista, I think. We can finally be rid of this place. It's not bad, but it's not for me or for her. Why are they not allowing her to meet her own friends? These people are not all good.

It all started when Pari said that she and her family are coming to Chennai. I kind of miss her and the children. I said we could all go back home, to Bella, for the time they are here.

I got quite excited about spending time in Bella. I can finally meet my friends, who have not yet removed me from the Bhakti Group, but I rarely understand their everyday chatter. Then, naturally, I imagined life there and realized I would miss Ammini. It was then that I realized she had nothing tying her here either. We could both simply move to Bella when Pari is here and then never leave. We are both really able to cook and clean and keep house.

I think it's a great idea. I will ask Ammini during our walk today.

Monday, 10 August 2015

Ammini doesn't seem to be for the idea of moving to Bella. So I did the next best thing: called Sekar. He wasn't enthusiastic either. I will keep talking about it. Maybe just invite Ammini for lunch when Pari is here. She'll see how wonderful it is there and then stay. She has to be with me — how can she not see that?

Tuesday, 11 August 2015

Pari has arrived. She came here to visit me. We'll go to Bella tomorrow, she said. Siva isn't here with her. Looks like she has brought a friend along.

They are all wearing name tags, like the staff. It's quite odd. They never gave Viswa any, I don't think. I wanted to introduce Ammini to them, but somehow we couldn't meet. No matter, she said she will think about coming to

Bella with me. I will convince her to come and they can meet then.

I noticed the funniest thing: Pari is not wearing her *thali*. I hope everything is okay between her and Siva. I'm guessing it's just one of those new things where they see it as some sort of bondage, the chain on your neck.

Palm Bella Vista, Chennai

Thursday, 13 August 2015

Suddenly, just now, it's enveloped me. Srini's gone.

I miss him here in this house. I miss his comments, his irritating swish–swash, his sincerity, his anger at the system, simply his presence. I wonder why. I am struck by loneliness, in spite of Viswa, Pari and the kids. I don't know what brought this about, but it's as if the power just came on. It's as if I'm looking through a microscope. I can recall, with great detail every little crease on his face, every little action, the way he looked when he was angry, the way he shook his head whenever politics took an ugly turn, the way his eyes shone when the match got interesting. I can hear his different tones clearly, as if he is standing right next to me: the base voice for official talk on the phone, the mid-tones for coffee, a little higher if he wanted sugar in his coffee, and the rare squeak for excitement. Of the cricket sort. If I close my eyes, I can almost see him sitting on the single-seater sofa, eyes fixed on the newspaper in his hand, the coffee tumbler–*davara* on the teapoy beside him, a snigger for every ridiculous piece of news he read.

I couldn't stop the tears from flowing. Was it some side effect of the medicines?

I wonder where Ammini is. I remember she said she would come along. I can't seem to find her when I need her the most.

It looks like the kids are planning a trip somewhere. I just want to be left here. Something about Pari's friend Radha seems familiar. I asked Viswa and all she said was, 'You don't remember?' and she hurriedly left the room.

Friday, 14 August 2015

What? Pari and Radha? And I've forgotten? I wonder what I am, now that it's clear I'm losing my memory, or my mind. What is a person if their memory is completely wiped out? No wonder people have been looking at me strangely.

How could I forget that? I think I need tattoos to remind me. Like that movie they showed on Sun TV. That one with the actor. I think I'll just talk less.

Saturday, 15 August 2015

I am stuffed. Literally.

The day started early with another speech by the prime minister.

Everyone was amused that I was watching it so early in the morning. Srini would usually watch it too, and I even made a flag-coloured lunch one year. I think the kids have forgotten it: carrot rice, coconut rice and pudina rice. It was when Rajiv Gandhi was prime minister. Maybe I'll try that again this year?

'Hey, Viswa,' I called out. She looked up from her cell phone.

I told her about my plan for lunch. She was so excited. 'Wow, Amma,' she said. 'I'll go get chips.'

How could they have forgotten that year? It was one of the highlights of my domesticity. They have no memory loss excuse.

'Call Sekar Chittappa and all also, no?' I suggested. It would be just like old times.

Around lunch time, the three of them came. Sekar, Renuka and Prathik. Renuka gave me a plastic cover with one kilo apples in them. Sekar and Prathik gave us huge smiles.

They played a movie and Radha seemed to know everyone. I remember who she is but realize it's only a matter of time before I forget again.

'Perima,' Prathik said to me. 'Remember how you forgot who I was at the home the other day?' He turned to Pari. 'Pari, she thought I was Appa's man-nurse!'

Pari stared at him and I smiled. 'Sorry, da,' I said in my nicest voice and Viswa joined her sister in staring at him angrily.

When the India flag rice was brought out, everyone went '*ooh*' and '*aah*' and I smiled.

'*Manni*, this again? I remember you made it way back and told us about it. Pari, you would have been, what, eight or nine, maybe?' Sekar said.

Someone remembered! I was overtaken by emotion. That it was Sekar was, well, expected, but also confusing. How did everyone else forget? Or, why did he remember?

The meal was made even more extensive by Radha's payasam ('No, it is not payasam, Aunty,' she explained several times. 'It is *kheer*.') Even so, I could not resist calling it 'payasam' when Prathik asked what it was. I suppose these are the cheap thrills of the memory challenged.

When everyone left, Srini's loss hit me again without warning. All of them asked what happened. All of them gave me looks of pity. A couple of them looked at their cell phones. I knew I could live like this forever, with all of them concerned about me. But the rest of them could not. Every single person had paused their lives to be with me.

Perhaps it was time to let them carry on to 'Cut the Rope', as the game was called.

I looked around and saw Ammini standing by the kitchen door. She had come, after all. How could I have forgotten her? I should have told the others that she would be eating here too. Why didn't she join us all? Or did she?

'Hey, why didn't you eat with us?' I asked, walking up to Ammini.

'Oh, you are all family. I didn't want to disturb you.'

'Oh, come on, you are more than family. Come, eat at least now. See, there is payasam also. Your favourite.'

'How can I eat alone?'

'What is all this formality?'

'I will feel lonely eating by myself.'

And that is how I ended up eating lunch twice today, and I feel my stomach will burst any time now.

Saturday, 22 August 2015

The kids are about to leave. I think I want to stay here, at home. I'm not sure I miss anything about the retirement centre. Maybe Ammini, if she returns, but she can simply stay with me, no?

Do you know the feeling of belonging that you feel when you're with people exactly like you? I have some time, so let me explain. Imagine a colony of bees. All they see are bees. All they imagine and dream are bees (and admittedly, flowers). They don't feel like bees, they feel like, I don't know, a worker, a drone or a queen. Now imagine a zoo. Or, even better, a farm. When the animals see other animals, the horses want to stay together. They feel like horses.

It's sort of like that. So when I am here in Bella I feel like I am an old person. There, at the old-age home, I feel like myself. Sometimes I feel like a lump of clay, but mostly like a person.

But I really want to stay with the kids. Pari and Viswa, that is. I want us to be back together as a family. I can conjure up Srini if I focus hard, so we can once again be the four of us. Five, with Ammini.

Wednesday, 26 August 2015

I am a mess. Not just the memory part, you see. I am a total and complete mess.

I am a mess because I never knew what I felt for my kids. Now I wonder if it's too late.

170

Pari and Radha are leaving in three days. I didn't respond to Radha when she called me 'Amma' and she learned to call me 'Aunty'.

What do I even know about relationships? The thought has been swirling around in my head for days. The other day they proved that I knew nothing.

One day, I saw them both on the sofa, a small gap between them, me watching them from the kitchen as they watched something on Star World. As the programme progressed, the distance between them grew shorter, and the programme was completely screened off. Radha's head was on Pari's shoulder. They must have seen my shadow, for they broke their link. Pari called me over, and led me to sit between them. They both leaned into my shoulder, like a proper triangle.

It was one of those moments in life when your heart seems to have melted, only to be moulded into a better version of itself. That was love. Love, confident in itself and not always looking over its shoulder for the enemy to appear. Love that gave as much as it took, not that it kept count. Love that was real. Love that could be whatever it wanted to be.

After this heart-melting moment, I examined myself. Try as I might, I often forgot that they were together. Or was I simply pretending? It becomes easier to pretend to lose memories when you're losing them anyway. Like when you cut onions and cry. Why, I made so many things with onions over the years.

171

Do I tell Pari that really, it wasn't their wedding that I minded or them together? Do I tell them that the wedding and the emotion of the first dance was likely not what pushed Srini off the edge? Was I brave enough to shift the burden of death from their shoulders to mine? Was I brave enough to tell Viswa that Pari's situation helped me pause her matrimonial hunt? That I wanted to freeze some part of the ever-changing ground beneath my feet, and maybe I sometimes amplify everything just so I can get my way?

Thank God for Ammini. When I lay down for my siesta, she came with an Amrutanjan Balm, and sat down and spoke to me. Suddenly, everything became clear.

Thursday, 27 August 2015

This morning I called Radha and Pari. I had already planned it all. They came, questions on their faces and name tags on their chests. I had made peace with the tags.

'Radha, Pari,' I began. 'I know I haven't really seemed to be supportive.'

Pari looked around, perhaps wanting to ensure her children saw this.

'I've not been supportive actually, about your wedding.'

Pari was still not looking at me.

172

'Pari, look at her,' Radha said, and somehow, magically, Pari did.

'So I'm sorry. It's not that I haven't had time to process this. It's…it's very complex. I really know you are made for each other and deserve all the support and happiness you can get.'

I gave them both a light hug.

'Radha, you are a wonderful woman,' I continued. 'I've seen how happy you have made Pari.'

'And, Pari,' I said winking, 'you totally do not deserve Radha.'

Pari was looking at me strangely. I reached back and took out my good tray. On it were two blouse pieces and a *vethala paaku*.

'It's the *mugam* and the *kalasam* for the Varalakshmi Viradham,' I explained to a confused Radha. 'It's a puja performed by a married woman for the prosperity of the entire family. You know, for money, happiness, babies…'

Radha was beaming. Pari snorted.

'Every year, on this day, the woman of the house performs the puja and makes an elaborate feast for the Goddess.'

I could hear Pari snigger but I continued, 'Srini's mother gave it to me, the older daughter-in-law, and by law it would go to the daughter-in-law of the family, so Prathik's would-be wife. But I want to give it to you. You are this family's older daughter-in-law.'

Radha bear hugged me as I finished, and the edge of the plate cut into my waist.

'I've told all my friends in the Bhakti group, and they will come here tomorrow evening for the formal *vethala paaku*.'

'Thank you, Aunty,' Radha said.

'Yes, it's time for everyone to know,' I said, and squeezed her hand.

'Lucky Prathik's wife,' Pari said.

'You can do your first puja tomorrow with my guidance and then carry it on from next year by yourself,' I told the girls. 'You can decide who is going to do it. You can too, Pari. Since we are breaking tradition anyway.'

'Oh, I have my period,' Pari replied instantaneously. 'It's got to be you, Rads.' She paused, adding, 'Forever.'

I looked back at Ammini, who was standing by the kitchen door, smiling. Thank God she had encouraged me to do this.

Vishnupuram Retirement Community, Chennai

Thursday, 1 October 2015

I am abandoning this journal project. Apparently, I'm making a lot of progress with the video games. Plus, I have Ammini. I haven't told Viswa about Ammini – she tends to get stressed out for some reason and follows it up with a dozen quack visits.

So I write only when I feel like it.

I'm back at the community. We, I mean. I told Ammini I will never let her go again.

Saturday, 7 November 2015

The rains have been horrible this year. The community is in a bit of a mess. Residents are not able to go out on walks and the mosquitoes are quite something. I've been feeling low all week. I don't know if it's the weather or the place or what. The only silver lining has been Ammini. Somehow though, I can't seem to see her often. I am holed up in my room a lot. She sometimes comes here, but I suppose she is not well for she hasn't come here in a long time.

I feel almost ready to leave this place, but I feel that something is missing. Like that time you go to the store and know that you're missing one item, but cannot remember what it is? Like that.

Maybe I'll go visit Sekar. If it were possible to exchange lives, I really would. I feel I have lived. Now, slowly, time is getting irritated with my persistence, like I'm Tendulkar on the crease, my time obviously over, refusing to make runs, refusing to get out.

Dark clouds have already gathered outside.

Wednesday, 2 December 2015

The floodgates have opened. The children have been asked to come and collect their parents if they want, as if school has shut early. But few can and fewer want to.

They have reorganized the rooms, so we're now sharing. Ammini is here with me. Her room is on the ground floor and she asked to be put up here with me, she said.

I watch from the large windows. It is as if She had come back for me.

As a child, I had offered Her Ammini, and as an adult, my mother-in-law. Now, She has come back for me. She has wanted me all along.

Friday, 4 December 2015

There is literally nothing for us to do. Our phone lines are cut and we have no power. I am writing this in the light of a candle. Some of us are huddled, two to three in a room.

These two days have been crystal clear in my head. The waters rising, the power shut down, the desperate calls, the old man who had to be transported to the hospital but couldn't make it. It's as if She has cornered us finally. Like a chess master, She is cutting off our options one by one.

Last night, I dreamed I was flailing, the floods of the Kollidam taking me away. All around me are high buildings, taller than the one I'm in now. People are free-falling down to the river, which winds its way through the landscape, man-made veins carrying the lifeblood to fields in the village and beyond. People are washed ashore to the fields, and I am thrown too. My eyes are closed, and blades of grass graze my nostrils.

I woke up breathless. All around me was darkness. For a minute I was disoriented. I opened the balcony door and could hear the water roar by. *Shhhhh*...like a terrible lullaby that puts the entire city to sleep, continually hushing up the cries for help.

I switched on the single torchlight in my room. Placing the torch in my mouth, I went back to the balcony where the rain spray wet my face. I switched off the torch and wiped my face clean, when a drop of water detached itself from the sunshade and dropped on my neck. It was like a thousand volts of electricity passed through me.

The memories came flooding in and I could not breathe. I needed to feel the elements on me. In me. I needed the rain, the water, the river. It seemed She had come to get me. Maybe I should go meet Her. From my perch on the fifth floor, all I could hear was Her roar. I felt Her calling me down to Her level, so that She could tell me a secret. She was calling out again now. I felt someone calling my name out loud. She could not take Ammini again – it had to be me.

As if on cue, Ammini got up.

'*Shhh*,' I said.

'She's calling for me,' Ammini said. She was shaking.

'*Shhh*. You cannot go now. She wants me. She has always wanted me.'

'No, no. It is me. The last time, She didn't get me. It's unfinished business She has with me. My Mother is calling me. I have to go.'

I reached out to stop her. I felt the heat coming from her, even from a distance. She was burning up.

'Ammini, you have fever.'

She laughed, a deep throaty laugh that was somehow preserved over the years. 'No, no, Pankajam, it's me, She wants me, let me go.'

I stood between her and the door.

'Let's both go, then. Let Her take who She wants.'

We stood there for a long time, staring at each other. Then slowly, we went slap-slapping down the stairs, side by side, hands linked.

We paused on the second floor.

'Are you sure?' Ammini asked me, and I nodded.

Everything was very dark and the only light came from my torch. We walked to the first floor and walked on, and reached the ground floor, where there was water all the way up to our waists. Mine, really. She was much shorter than me, so it reached nearly up to her chest. We had no idea where to go, but we moved ahead. It was as if a strange force led us by hand.

We passed the garden, feeling our way through the water. We walked past the play court, the lawn, the barely used swimming pool. I allowed myself a smile, then panicked, and smiled again. I really did not know where the pool began, but it didn't matter. She could choose whom She wanted. The water was indeed attracting me, for better or for worse.

'Come on,' I shouted to the water raining from above and rising from below. 'Come and get me. Let Ammini go.' As we walked closer to the 'Out' gate, I realized Ammini was at a disadvantage. She was so much shorter than me.

Water was gushing out of our compound, joining other angry streams. Dirty, stinking, furious. Furious, for we had not listened to Her. I imagined Her droplets of water, joining into one angry mob, like the people in *Gandhi*. Plastic covers, garbage, sanitary pads and diapers, with their attendant smells, were all part of the mix. They were all being washed away in the Great Cleansing.

Suddenly, the torchlight went off. I held my hand out for Ammini but could not feel her.

'Ammini,' I shouted, as loud as I could, but did not hear back. All I heard was the swooshing water in response. But no Ammini. I waited in the dark, hands outstretched, feeling this way and that, calling out my friend's name. When my arms started to ache, I lowered them and continued shouting. After a while I stopped that too, simply standing in the rain. My mind raced back towards another year, another storm, another powerless night.

The sky was darker than it had ever been, and it seemed angry. Angry at me. Nerves of steel flashed before the angry rumbles. My mother-in-law's moans punctuated the spectacle. It was as if she was commanding them to scare me.

Granted, I did not run to my mother-in-law the second she called from the bed she had been confined to for the past month or so. Granted, I spent more time talking to Sekar than I did Srini. Granted, I was not entirely unhappy when Srini had to leave town for official work, like he had that day. The winds howled and the trees swayed, and it seemed she was reaching for me through the rains in a way she could not by herself.

She had somehow summoned our Kollidam, it seemed — the Kollidam who had reached out for Ammini through land and was now reaching out for me through the skies.

A sudden crackle of thunder sent me running back to the house, straight into Sekar's arms. He held me while I sobbed, for the first time. His touch at the back of my neck was like cool water. Goosebumps sprouted all over.

He hushed me as my sobs slowed down, even as my heart rate shot up. He kissed the top of my head and I looked up at him. In the dark, all that was visible was his profile — his jawbone set sharper than his brother's, and his eyes, a shade browner.

His finger traced a line along my nose and my mouth, and I bit his finger that dared to touch my lips. He replaced his finger with his mouth and I took it hungrily. As my hands explored his back and his mine, I knew this was what my body and soul had been waiting for. We went to the bedroom without a word.

Afterwards, as I buttoned my blouse, I whispered, 'Go away, Sekar.'

'*Manni*,' he gasped. 'Pankajam.' I winced at my name off his tongue.

The name, soft and sweet, seemed like the calm centre of a cyclone raging in my mother-in-law's urgent moans, itself enveloped within the raging storm outside.

'Go away,' I hissed.

'You want this, and I do too.'

'We should not have. What have I done? What have I done?'

'It's what have *we* done, Pankajam.'

'How could you do this to your brother?'

He glared at me. 'Brother? You are his wife! And well, it seems destined. You...'

'I know I started it,' I snapped.

'Pankajam, Pankajam. I'm not talking about just this,' he said. 'But the rest of it too.'

I hated that I loved how my name sounded when he said it. I remember shaking my head. The rain, now angrier, slapped a loose window repeatedly.

He knelt in front of me, by the bed. 'Pankajam,' he said, 'We are perfect for each other. You know it. Even if we never had this, what just happened, we just...fit.'

I remained silent.

'You talk all about real freedom for the woman. The real thing, not an edited version. So here it is. We can do whatever *you* want. We can go away, where we can live a happy life. You know we want this, the two of us. Or you can continue to live here with Srini. The choice is entirely yours. I want to be with you, of course.'

I said nothing. I knew this was my chance. Yet, something stopped me. Maybe it was the lashing rain or my racing heart. Maybe it was just that I was scared of the depths within those eyes. Or that I so desperately wanted to run, run, run away with this man, wherever my feet would take me, heedless of any damage I might do to others. Just like Her.

No, no. That would not do. I looked outside, as the rain seemed to take a breather. I could not possibly damage everything in my path. Human beings were meant to be rational, not like wayward rivers, flooding and drying up as they pleased. It was dangerous, this following your heart. And Srini. Sweet, sweet Srini.

I had decided: After this night, we would continue life as before, as if this were a dream. Why, I convinced myself it was. I pushed that night as far back as it would go, like a hidden roll of emergency cash. Yes, that is where it would reside forever.

A month later, we had my mother-in-law's *subham*.[17]

Flashes of the past crept by: me crying on the desk in our room, when Sekar said 'yes' to Renuka. Me grimacing every time I saw Renuka and Sekar together. Crying through my pregnancy. Srini, calm as ever, proposing we move out for my good health. Me, agreeing, a stone in my heart. Srini, taking charge of the pregnancy and the baby Parineeta. Suddenly, the tableau stopped. Just black.

My mind was in a whirl. My body waited for deliverance.

I stayed that way, getting wet, until darkness slowly gave way to light. I looked in all directions, but even before all of this, I knew, just knew, that She had taken Ammini away, once again. And once again, I had been spared. Or had I? I thought I heard a loud crack of thunder, like a whip on my back.

I began the long walk back home.

17. The happy ending. In this case, the ascent of the soul to heaven.

184

ACKNOWLEDGEMENTS

Grateful to (in no particular order):

- Goddess Saraswati, who decided to visit me, even if in a suspected case of mistaken identity.
- Mahalakshmi, the more creative one, always; and Vivek, for opening up worlds I couldn't have possibly imagined.
- Kanima, Aarthi, Janaki and Sathya, the pillars who hold my home aloft as I escape into my own world.
- My own coven – Praveena Shivram and Amritha Dinesh – forever the wind beneath my broom.
- Parents who opened up their lives and hearts.
- Members of Writing in India, a writing-related flea market like none other.
- Appa, for the freedom to soar.
- Writer's Ink and its members – especially Bragadeesh Prasanna, Fehmida Zakeer, and its founder, Radhika Meganathan; and friends Vrinda Baliga and Ganesh Vancheeswaran for their generous inputs.

- Dr M. Santhana Krishnan, FRCPsych, old age psychiatrist, UK, who answered my queries patiently.
- Nalini Balachander for opening her home to host a lovely writer's retreatweekend.
- The Mantri Developers team for delaying our housing project so much that I had no neighbours to distract me from writing.
- Friends from the Sans Serif Book Club for their razor-sharp conversations on life, literature and everything in between.
- My agent, Kanishka Gupta.
- My editor, Cibani Premkumar, for her fine sculpting of the manuscript.
- Poulomi Chatterjee and the entire team at Hachette India for their trust in the book.
- Sahana and Siddharth, for the everyday reality checks.
- Vijay,for being The Rock (I sometimes hit my head against); and
- Amma, for everything.